James was born in London in 1936 where he experienced the outbreak of the Second World War. In 1941, he was taken to Canada and educated there and in the US. Upon graduation he worked as a map surveyor in the Canadian arctic. The land was surveyed for map making during the winter months as it was easier to traverse and measure the distance. James learned the ways of the north by living with the Cree Indians. He walked on snowshoes and many days covered over 50 miles in -70°F weather. He camped out in a tent, cooked over a wood fire, which he started without matches, a skill he learnt from the Cree and boiled snow for water. After his northern adventures and further worldwide travelling, he established a chain of retail stores selling sheepskins and homemade goods. A few decades later, he returned to the UK and settled on a farm.

Call of the Wild, a book by Jack London, inspired and set me on course for a life of adventure.

'There is nothing quite like being alone with nature deep in the middle of nowhere with only yourself to depend on.'

I dedicate, *Lionheart* to all living things.

– James Wild

James L. Wild

Lionheart: A Beacon Of Hope

Austin Macauley Publishers™
London • Cambridge • New York • Sharjah

A CIP catalogue record for this title is available from the British Library.

ISBN 9781035844289 (Paperback)
ISBN 9781035844296 (Hardback)
ISBN 9781035844302 (ePub e-book)

www.austinmacauley.com

First Published 2024
Austin Macauley Publishers Ltd®
1 Canada Square
Canary Wharf
London
E14 5AA

Ann Hedges who contacted various publishers and supported me in my application.

Thank you

Table of Contents

My perilous journey begins long ago,
A soul awakened, an unseen spark,
To venture forth, to discover, to know,
A passage through the dark.

In the Beginning...

Once upon a time, in the not-too-distant past, a light travelled throughout the universe, searching for a heartbeat worthy of a star. A shallow mountain stream, on a blue terrestrial globe, attracted the light and discreetly channelled its path. And so began the extraordinary relationship of a small finite being to a source of light and energy that knew no bounds or limits.

The voice of the stream was as faint as a whisper, its spirit lifted with each new awakening. A sleepy underwater world stirred to a rhapsody of colour. Deliciously idle, the water sparkled with all the purity of nature's first day. Into this vibrant domain a fragile life form appeared, unlocked its vision and became aware of light.

With clockwork precision, new and untried life emerged and took their chance with existence. All that is except one – the one touched by the light. For this little entrant had woken to a different tune and felt ill at ease with its earthly presence. The other newborns knew exactly what to do and did so unaware of what they were, unimpressed by where they were and oblivious to the trials that lay ahead. With each passing day, however, the one touched by the light grew more restless and apprehensive. It had no idea of what or who it was and the effect on its consciousness was so bewildering that it hesitated to venture out into this strange, underwater world.

The streamlet's outer look of peace and tranquillity disguised the struggle taking place within. A labyrinth of hidden threats and terrors confronted each new arrival. Not only were they easy prey for roving predators but also sport for fickle currents and unexpected storms. They seemed as helpless as flowers born in a tempest, delicate petals clinging to life on the end of a windblown stem. Yet they all possessed an intense desire to exist, which more than made up for their limitations.

Minute in size, these micro-organisms were programmed to be fish – a distinct species of marine life known as salmon. Incapable of thought, they knew without thinking how to swim and fend for themselves. Within days every grain, every pebble, every nook and cranny of their natal stream became familiar. For the stream meant home and its precise location would be fixed in their minds until later engaged to help seal their destiny. They need never give thought to ocean tides or the moon's eclipses by which their lives were regulated. This was true for all except the one touched by the light. Underfed and undersized it gave the impression that it belonged to a lower order of creation. From the outset, it swam with a gracelessness that shamed its fellow kind and its inability to care for itself made it a target of abuse. These obvious shortcomings clouded its outlook and lowered its self-esteem. This set it apart from the others, causing it to be awkward and shy. It soon became so stressed and discombobulated that it couldn't tell friend from foe or even the correct food to eat and therefore ill-equipped to deal with life's unending challenge. It stood on the brink of extinction. Its fellow kind referred to it as the outsider, but behind its back they whispered the word, “misfit”. They considered it an oddity or some form of miscreation. Before long, its presence began to offend them, and so they ignored it altogether. Isolated and ridiculed it kept to itself, its eyes cast down in shame.

The truth, of course, was far from simple. The outcast came into existence severely disadvantaged. For it lacked the basic skills necessary to compete with its environment. And the reason was plain to see – its natural or inborn instinct was defective. And so, rejected and dejected, it suffered alone in silence. Nonetheless, as it fought and struggled to stay alive the unwillingness of its fellow kind to rally round and lend support caused events that could not be foreseen. For one fateful day, to the outcast’s shock and surprise, the light of awareness ignited and in less than a heartbeat its outlook changed. It recognized, for the first time, the need to adapt or cease to exist and felt compelled to observe and learn from its fellow kind. Through hard work and devotion to purpose it managed to hold its own. By trial and error, gaining from success as well as failure, the seed of curiosity was sown and rapidly took root.

Due to its questioning mind and capacity to absorb information the outcast developed a unique and exceptional intelligence. It understood that it could count on no one but itself, that it was abandoned and alone in the midst of infinite danger, without help and with no other aim than the one it set for itself.

Early one day, the stream brimmed with excitement. The new arrivals had steadily matured, reaching a state of extraordinary agitation. Overnight they’d been struck and overcome by the spirit of adventure, forcing them to breach their limits. Intuitively, they merged with the outgoing flow, surrendering to the power of instinct.

The dawning light winked and blinked through pink-tinted clouds. Rippling water skipped merrily along as it weaved its way between reed-fringed shores and woodland green. The infant salmon were ferried over sand and pebble stone, through clusters of sun-blest flora and past slumbering beds of incubating life. The stream murmured softly to the rhythm of rising birdsong. Early morning sunrays lanced its crystal flow, creating magical prisms of colour. The rider's blended invisibly – silver gleams within the stream. In quiet momentum the drift gradually broadened, deepened and finally yielded to a glacial lake; its living cargo safely delivered to a wide-open expanse of water. Unnoticed, the outcast trailed along behind.

Sunbeams filtered down through pale green waters, igniting shadowy things that flashed and clashed. Fierce individuals patrolled exclusive territories, always on the prowl for weaker kinds. Danger pressed from all directions. Silvery blurs scribbled the water as swarms of small fry dashed for food, then scattered like sparks when the strong swept in to swell their gullets. Deeper down, the sunless depths bristled with more menacing threats. Hidden eyes left nothing unwatched. Constant harassment kept the newcomers on the sharp edge and those unwary soon perished. Existence meant struggle and pain and sudden extinction.

In a desperate moment, the outcast cried out, 'If I'm so soon done, why was I begun?' It now found itself in a great body of water stocked with fierce and frightful creatures, where most were hunters and all were prey. To add to the terrors, raptorial birds were constantly on the wing, skimming the waves and plucking victims from down beneath the surface. Yet, strange to say, a faint whisper from a source within eased its anxious mind:

Nothing can ever harm you,
For I am what you will become,
And when darkness falls,
Look to the light.

Thus, despite hungry eyes and open mouths, the outcast persevered and survived.

And so, life carried on. Now and then the outcast would leave its hideout to forage food with those of its own size. It chose this group rather than larger more aggressive types and end up their prey. On one such occurrence, a recent new arrival approached. Upon noting the outcast's quirky style, it sniggered, 'I see swimming isn't one of your strong points, hahahaha! My name is Fyn, with a "y". I am a Salmon fish and a member of the Coho family,' he boasted, proudly.

'What is your name and what family do you belong to?'

But the outcast didn't know if it had a name, let alone a family to belong to. So, it quickly gulped its meal, swallowed its pride and hastened off to its hiding place. In low spirits, it withdrew into the shadows. Silent and out-of-sight it consumed its time immersed in fear, in doubt, yet full of wonder, dreaming dreams no mortal ever dared to dream.

The seasons changed then changed again. The outcast grew more restless and curious. With eyes deep in thought, it often paused to ponder the tangled mysteries of life. Its inquisitive mind searched and wrestled with the wonders and strangeness of existence and, as a result, the following thought took flight …

'I never cease to wonder,
At being here and now,
And often pause to ponder,
The reasons why and how.'

and directly, a still, small voice replied, 'when the heart is ready the teacher will appear!'

Brief Encounter

'A member of the universe'

A thick blanket of fog layered the lake, obscuring the landscape. Through a shimmering haze of mist, a brilliant rainbow flared. Soon after, a great white Swan emerged and observed the outcast, gulping down a string of gnats. The Swan's tapered head housed intense blue eyes that held their target without moving. Pins of light bounced off its pure white feathers. Ghostlike, it glided serenely through the mist towards the little outcast, its long, elegant neck leaning out, then freezing. The perfect eyes locked onto the outcast. The outcast froze in mid-gulp. The Swan's intelligent eyes revealed a depth of tenderness, a characteristic that put the outcast at ease. A tense moment followed before the Swan spoke:

'Be not afraid, my friend – I am on your side,' the stranger greeted.

'My name is Oranos and I appear as a Swan. I spend most of my time as a wandering spirit in the clouds above. In my sweep and soar over earth-bound souls, I heard your cries of despair. I'm here to mend your wounded spirit and help you find your inner *Self,* the light that comes to the darkness.'

The outcast stared in stunned disbelief, utterly speechless. In a small, tremulous voice, it stuttered, 'wh-wh-what is l-light?'

'Light is the radiant energy that connects you to the universe. Its power is unlimited – its source, inexhaustible – its presence, unseen. Although you cannot grasp it – it touches you always – within your reach and yet beyond and as vague as the shadow of a breath of air. It is your unlearned behaviour impelled from within – it is your guiding light – it is your dearest and closest friend.'

Totally bewildered, the outcast simply stared at the Swan, its eyes crowded with questions. *How strange*, it thought, *to be here in the middle of a lake, conversing with a great white Swan.* And then he wondered why the Swan's mouth never moved when it spoke – yet the sound of its voice was resonate and compelling. Somehow the words were transmitted through thought – understood by no one except the intended recipient!

Mastering its shyness, the outcast asked, 'Please tell me, what is a guiding light?'

'A guiding light is many things and more,' said Oranos, 'it is your heart – your mind – your spirit – your soul – the force within that links you to the source – it is your indwelling *Self* – the smartest and deepest part of you and by far the hardest and most difficult to know,' explained the Swan. 'To help you discover and know your *Self* you are destined to experience a life full of meaning – a life of high adventure and great achievement – a life filled with challenge.' The swan paused momentarily to allow the outcast to grasp his words. He then explained further: 'an ocean of truths lies before you, each waiting to be discovered – once made known the impact will be profound. You have a great mission to accomplish – a great role to play. To this end you have entered the world as a super-class Pisces – a marine creature of the salmon species – and a dearly loved and cherished member of the universe.'

'Is that who I am – a salmon fish!' exclaimed the outcast with a hint of relief.

'That is *what* you are – not *who* you are. You have yet to discover who you are. Today you are a child of light unschooled in the ways of life – a disconnected soul. Your tomorrows are yet to be. There is much to learn. Life will take you from unknown to unknown, each moment filled with wonder – each moment charged with mystery. In your struggle to prevail, you will be sorely tested. If you do not succumb but rise to overcome, you will go where your spirit can express itself in unlimited freedom. To succeed you must broaden the scope of your horizons – extend the depth of your vision – see more in you than you think there is to be seen.'

'I feel so alone and afraid,' confessed the little salmon. 'No one cares or wants to be my friend. I am scorned and shunned. I don't know why I'm here or what to do,' he anguished in dismay. 'What's to become of me? I seem to count for nothing,' disheartened and discouraged, he rambled on. 'I've tried so hard to make sense of it all – to make sense of me! What is the purpose of life?' The hapless little creature emptied his heart to the Swan, pouring out all his pent up hurt and frustration.

'I know how lonely and frightened you are,' replied Oranos, kindly. 'But you are not alone. Help is standing by. You are as you are for a special purpose. Do not let others shame you for this. Don't let your past dictate who you are, but let it be part of what you will become.'

‘Why is life so complicated?’ sighed the outcast. ‘And so unfair?’

‘Right now, that may appear to be true,’ said Oranos. ‘But what you believe as unfortunate happenings are the first moves in achieving your destiny. Listen closely and watch carefully for the journey ahead is long and perilous, fraught with real and imagined dangers with every sweep of your tail. Know that Nature never punishes, she always teaches – be grateful for the difficult times, for in those you grow in wisdom – recognize, the tragedy of life does not lie in not reaching your goal but in having no goal to reach – and above all, know that nothing in this world is possible without adversity. Even so, every moment in life is precious and to those who understand, life is a miracle. From this day forward, you shall be known as Sami, the Warrior of the Light.’ Oranos then dipped his head beneath the surface and looked deep into the youngster’s eyes, ‘Sami, you are not what you are born, but what you have it in you to be. You will never be satisfied until you know the truth of who you are. Do not squander the treasure of your birth.’

Upon these words, the Swan raised his head, swept his wings and vanished into the misty, rainbowed sky.

The brief encounter left the little salmon thunderstruck. Surprisingly, he felt an unexpected warmth of contentment. Something new and wonderful was opening within, some strange happening. But most remarkable and truly uplifting, he sensed his doubts and fears were losing their grip. As he hurried on his way, he thought to himself, *I am a super-class Pisces – a marine creature of the salmon species – and Sami is my name*. And with a show of confidence, he proudly proclaimed, ‘the universe is my family!’

Early next day, Sami was up and about, trolling for gnats. The soft morning light lay about him in a wash of coloured tints. Clouds of freshly hatched flies danced dizzily above the surface. Fyn soon turned up, well fed and looking pleased with life. On spotting Sami, his eyes expressed amazement. The once clumsy swimmer showed definite signs of improvement – even a dash of flair!

The Difference Maker

'A bright new future'

A solitary dragonfly hovered like a pale ghost against the blue of the sky. When Sami split the surface to swallow the tasty critter, to his surprise, he was met by a friendly greeting: 'Good day to you, Sami! Welcome to a bright new future!'

Sami froze in mid-leap. He stared with startled, outsized eyes at a most unusual creature, a giant double-winged fly. As it hovered above, Sami carefully checked it over. Attached to its long tubular frame were four gossamer wings that hummed with a high-speed velocity – its fine delicate body glittered like emerald-blue sequins – two multifaceted eyes dominated its tiny head – and, as it hung suspended in mid-air, a gold-threaded haze circled round its presence. But most intriguing and indeed, surprising – its 'words' were delivered unspoken, exactly like the Swan.

Sami gave the winged stranger a quizzical look. 'Who are you?' he asked in a hesitant voice. 'And what do you mean by 'bright new future'?'

'I am known as the difference-maker,' the stranger announced. 'I have come from far beyond the horizon – far beyond the realms of reality. I appear as a dragonfly. I am here to unlock your potential and prepare you for your destiny.

You can call me, Apollo. Consider me your friend and mentor. I shall act as your guardian angel – I am your guiding light.'

A dragonfly – my guiding light! How strange! thought Sami. Then out of curiosity, he asked, 'How did you know my name?'

'The Swan, Oranos, brought your concerns to me,' replied the dragonfly.

'I met the Swan only yesterday,' recalled Sami. 'He mentioned my destiny and also spoke of a journey.'

'Everyone, without exception, undergoes a journey and no one is excluded,' explained Apollo. 'A journey is best described as a lifelong adventure. It begins at the time of birth and ends when its time is done.'

'You mean my journey has already begun!' exclaimed Sami. 'Then what is a destiny?' he asked, 'please explain?'

'A destiny is a predetermined course of events beyond your powers to resist,' Apollo replied. 'It is a purpose – a goal to strive for – a mission to accomplish.'

These answers only raised more questions, adding to Sami's confusion. While he tried to grasp the meaning of the words "journey" and "destiny", Apollo hovered close to the surface. As the dragonfly drew near, Sami was struck by the piercing brilliance of its eyes. They were sharp and impressive, which suggested a higher intelligence, comparable to the swan.

Perched atop a lofty lake-weed, Apollo commenced to make clear his mission and impress upon Sami the realities of his situation: 'to begin with Sami, your doubts and fears are not sent in vain. They force you to think hard and deep in search of solutions. You must also forget what you think you are and accept the way you really are – and don't become a slave to your past.' The dragonfly paused briefly before he continued: 'as we team up to work together always be positive and never doubt that with my assistance and your persistence, we shall solve the mystery of your existence.' After agreeing to meet early next day, the dragonfly gave a crisp little nod and promptly disappeared.

Sami felt completely at ease in the dragonfly's presence. And it wasn't just because of their size difference. It was much more than that. Somehow, he sensed a long-lost friend had magically turned up.

Early next day the eagle, Horus, sailed the currents of the sky. His far-seeing eyes probed the mirrored lake below. Upon spotting Sami chasing sun sparkles, he called out:

'Run free little one,
Run free,
Your destiny lies in the sky,
The sky,
Your destiny lies in the sky.'

In high spirits, Sami flashed like wet silver as he leapfrogged in and out of the water. It wasn't long before Sami heard his name called and halted play.

Apollo had been skimming the surface, sizing up Sami's aquatic skills. 'Good day to you, Sami,' he greeted. 'Your last jump wasn't too bad. It definitely showed promise. But you'll have to jump a lot higher if you expect to achieve your destiny.'

'You mentioned my destiny yesterday,' said Sami. 'Please, tell me more?' he pressed. 'You told me you're here to prepare me for it!'

'That's right, Sami. I've come to prepare you for your journey and help you achieve your destiny. But it is for you alone to bring to light and make happen, not me. I can only advise and prepare you. At journey's end you'll find the answers you seek,' he explained, vaguely. 'At that time, you'll discover who you are. If successful you'll be rewarded beyond your wildest dreams and become an inspiration to us all.'

Sami looked doubtful. 'Is my journey far? Is it difficult?'

'It's impossible to say,' said Apollo. 'Every journey is different – no two are alike. Each presents its own challenge.'

Within easy earshot, a humble hermit crab raised one of its claws to draw attention. In a voice more imposing than its size, the crab said: 'Oh little salmon fry, listen to my words of wisdom. Learning is a daring and endless adventure. But to gain knowledge and understanding you must first equip yourself with doubt. For doubt breeds questions, and questions demand answers.' The crab then lowered its claw and sidled closer to Sami: 'your future is filled with tomorrows, each waiting to become today. What tomorrow holds you cannot predict but you can prepare for its uncertainties by making today all that it can be.' After a thoughtful moment, the crab went on to say: 'you're too young, Sami, to have learned the intensity of understanding that can only come through adversity. The truth you seek is shrouded in secrecy and cannot be found without erring first. You must learn from your own mistakes. Turn misfortune into fortune. To go wrong in your own way is better than to go right in someone else's.'

Sami wriggled his fins in puzzlement and asked, 'What is truth and where can I find it?'

'Truth can be found in everything and everywhere,' replied the crab, ambiguously. 'You just have to open your mind and know where and how to look.'

This response left Sami more baffled than ever. With all these new and strange ideas confronting him, how could he be sure of anything? Unless he was able to swim and jump beyond his present means, he'd never complete his journey and would never know his destiny. And what about truth! He could only guess what that meant! 'Why does life have to be so difficult?' he wondered. 'And why won't anyone tell me what my destiny is and why it's so important?'

While Sami gave thought to these questions, the crab spoke out again. This time he introduced himself as Homer, and mindful of Sami's frustration offered a few words of advice: 'if you only swim in tranquil waters, you'll never find the truth.' And after a reflective moment, he said: *'Always head towards what you seek!'* Sami looked even more confused. And so, in a confiding whisper, Homer revealed: '*In the heart of every being, where the quiet mind can hear, there speaks a silent voice, and the voice is never untrue.'* And on a lighter note, he added: 'cheer up, Sami – exercise your mind – try solving this knotty brainteaser: *yesterday is history – tomorrow is a mystery – and today? Today is a gift. That's why it's called the present* … in the meantime, Sami, listen to Apollo, for his words ring true.'

Preparation

'Fail to prepare – prepare to fail'

The rising sun cast its early rays upon the lake, gilding a frisky salmon in shades of gold. Sami was busy chasing swarms of gnats while keeping a sharp lookout for the dragonfly. Before long, Apollo appeared, hovering overhead.

'Today, I have a big surprise for you, Sami,' announced an upbeat Apollo. 'You're due to meet one of the wonders of the water-world – a fellow marine creature renowned for his aquatic skills. He's agreed to show you how to master the skills necessary to become a potent and effective swimmer. He'll show you how to power-kick your tail – how to work your fins to advantage and how to navigate vast oceans and manoeuvre through aggressive waters. By faithfully following his lessons, you'll reshape your body, making it more streamlined and hydrodynamic. This will reduce water drag and save on energy and muscle strain thus enabling you to cover vast distance over long periods of time. But most important and fundamental to your success, he'll teach you how to develop and strengthen your tail muscles, allowing you to jump and overleap seemingly impossible obstacles.'

To Sami this all sounded a bit too much. He wondered how a dragonfly could possibly know anything about life underwater, let alone swimming! 'I'm not sure about taking lessons,' he said. 'I don't think I need to be taught how to swim. After all, I swim a lot better than I used to. I get by pretty well as I am.'

'Contrary to what you think you know, Sami, I began life underwater – I spent my early days there. So, I know what I'm talking about. But I'm not here to discuss me. I'm here for you and your future only,' explained Apollo. 'To just *get by,* Sami, is not good enough. Think of your body as a loyal and magic partner and by working together in harmony with your mind you can accomplish anything. But first your body must be schooled and trained in the right way. Don't waste what you have, Sami – don't waste your life on limitations.'

'But I can swim fairly well now,' argued Sami. 'Anyway, why should I take lessons? I'll never be as good as the others.'

Apollo refused to indulge in Sami's low self-esteem. 'Look,' he said, 'it'll be hard enough for you to succeed without defeating yourself before you've started. You never know what you can do until you've tried. Success does not happen overnight. Patience becomes a part of learning.' The dragonfly paused for a moment to gather his thoughts and then added: 'as you journey through life Sami, fate, circumstance, and other things will at times be almost overwhelming against you. You can only succeed if you don't condemn yourself from the start. If you have no faith in yourself, then who will? I won't. I wouldn't waste my time, and neither will anyone else. Do you understand?'

Duly chastised and feeling foolish, Sami meekly apologized, 'Sorry,' he muttered.

'I accept your apology,' acknowledged Apollo. 'But first you must accept that I cannot help you unless you're prepared to help yourself. Now listen closely and repeat after me: *I am strong – I am not weak – I am strong – I am not weak!'*

To appease Apollo, Sami agreed to repeat the words. Apart from anything else, deep down, he hoped to equal if not outpace his fellow kind. '*I am strong – I am not weak – I am strong – I am not weak,'* he repeated.

'Keep those words in the forefront of your mind and whenever in doubt say them to yourself – repeat them over and over again until they become part of you,' stressed Apollo. 'As you make your way through life, Sami, you'll meet adversity wherever you go. So, don't face the future unprepared.' The dragonfly paused briefly to arrange his thoughts: 'Today you'll see skills you've never seen before – skills that you'll need to help you reach your goal and achieve your destiny. An aquatic expert will soon arrive to demonstrate how best to employ these skills. Then it's up to you to master and put them to active use. With dedication and day-to-day practice skills sharpen – confidence builds – and *self-belief* takes hold. You cannot succeed, Sami, however hard you try, unless you trust and believe in your *Self.* Do not think otherwise. Success depends on you and you alone. So, it's in your *Self*-interest to pursue excellence and be the best that you can be. Much good will follow. Now it's a matter of urgency, for soon you'll be on your way. Time is running short.'

The dragonfly's concern was unmistakable, which made a deep impression on Sami. So, he agreed to go along with the lessons. 'I'll do my best,' he promised.

'That's all I ask,' said Apollo. 'Everyone, at some point, needs help.'

'When do I start my lessons?'

‘First of all, Sami, empty your mind of everything you think you know about swimming – and then we’ll start from the beginning. Your …’

‘Excuse me,’ interrupted Sami. ‘Who is to be my teacher?’

‘Be patient, Sami. I was just about to tell you,’ replied Apollo. ‘Your teacher is a river otter by the name of Loki. You’ll like him.’

‘Hang on!’ cried Sami, alarmed. ‘An otter will eat me alive! We’re born enemies!’

‘You’ve nothing to fear,’ assured Apollo. ‘Loki has come as a friend not a foe. Recognize that under the natural laws of planet Earth I’d be considered your prey, not your mentor. Celestial law governs us now. So put your mind at ease. Accept Loki as a friend and take advantage of his expertise. You’ll benefit enormously. But first and foremost, you must learn the basic skills and then develop them through day-to-day use. The trials you face are physical and demanding and require the utmost in strength and endurance.’

‘Yes, but please tell me.’

‘Tell you what?’

‘How can an otter teach me how to swim?’

‘Wait and see, Sami, you’ll be impressed,’ said Apollo. ‘Loki is not only here to teach what you want to know but what you need to know. Skill acquisition is a compulsory requirement. I cannot stress strong enough how important this is. Your destiny depends on it. To qualify as an expert requires dedication and hard work. But dedication and hard work do not go unrewarded – for the benefits gained are substantial and justify the sacrifice. Remember Sami, anything you learn in life, that’s worthwhile, exacts a price. During your time spent training you'll also need to practice self-control and suppress your natural desires. This allows you to channel all your energy into achieving perfection. As your skills become part of you and you start to enjoy success, you'll have to fight the urge to relax in self-satisfaction. So, it won't be easy. But the way to get there is through practice, practice, and more practice – practice until the skills become second nature, till you feel you're born with them. Do the simple things well and the rest will follow. And always try to do better than your best and never be content with a low standard when a higher one can be achieved with a little more effort. Remember, you can train hard, fight easy and win, or you can train easy, fight hard and lose. The choice is yours. But if you fail to prepare – prepare to fail. What Loki and I cannot teach you is courage – that's something you'll have to find on your own.'

'What's courage?' asked Sami. 'Must I be tough?'

'Mentally tough, yes – but tough on its own is not enough,' replied Apollo. 'Courage is your lifeblood, Sami – it calls for willpower, tenacity and resolve. Without courage you cannot succeed.'

Try as he would, Sami could find no connection between him and courage. Nevertheless, being naturally curious and open-minded he waived his concerns and agreed to meet the otter.

Without warning, a streaking shadow skewered the lake and burst through the surface calm. Sami's eyes widened in disbelief as they tracked a blurry figure execute an astonishing double aerial somersault and then re-enter the lake with a splash less dive. Before he could catch his breath, he was face to face with a be-whiskered, puppy-eyed sensation, glistening all-over with fur. Sami stared in amazement. Mischievous eyes stared right back. After a tense moment the aquatic marvel flipped over on his back, locked Sami in a twinkling gaze, and cheerfully introduced himself.

'Hi Sami. Give us a smile – you're looking at Loki!'

With a nod and a wink, Loki commenced to demonstrate his extraordinary talent. With effortless ease, he slipped through the water with the style and grace of a prima ballerina and performed such spectacular leaps and rolls that Sami couldn't help but be impressed. It wasn't hard to see why Loki, with his uncanny skills and infectious good nature, helped make the world a more agreeable place. It was clear that Sami not only liked Loki but admired him.

Apollo hovered in the air nearby. 'Good to see you again, Loki.'

Sami desperately wanted to measure up to the otter's performance but in wake of Loki's energy and incredible flourish had misgivings about his abilities. He also lacked the courage to try. Noting Sami's reluctance, the otter continued his acrobatic play and finished by swimming rings around the startled novice.

'Pretty impressive, eh?' grinned Loki.

'Brilliant!' agreed Sami. 'But if you don't mind, I think I'll just watch for now. Perhaps I'll join you later.'

'Mere watching may help you understand, Sami, but doing allows you to know,' prompted Apollo. 'If you've never faced failure, you'll never know success. So don't underestimate yourself. No one knows their limits until they've tried.'

'Pretend it's a game and do as I do,' encouraged Loki. 'C'mon Sami, give it a try – follow me!'

Sami cautiously followed the otter. Both headed towards the middle of the lake, their pace gradually picking up. Then Loki swung sharply to the left and Sami did the same. Sami was enjoying the chase when all at once the otter arched his back, kicked his tail and shot straight up through the surface. Airborne and free of restraint, he completed a flawless, mid-air, backward spinning cartwheel. Sami did his best to duplicate the feat and as he broke the surface and kicked into the air, he was thrilled to see that he'd never jumped so high before. The thrill was quickly lost, however, when the belly flopped with a loud splash.

'All you need is a little practice,' encouraged Loki. 'Remember, your best teacher is your last mistake.'

From then on, for the next season or so, the otter and his pupil were seldom seen apart. Sami never faltered in his pursuit of excellence. Every day brought him closer to perfection. After one exhilarating and exceptional workout, a tired but enthused Sami could not contain his curiosity; 'Please tell me Loki,' he asked, 'what is my destiny?'

'All in good time,' answered Loki. 'Like Apollo said it differs for each of us and is for you alone to bring to light. Be patient and don't worry – hard work and dedication will get you there in the end. But be in no doubt Sami, you cannot escape from who you are. Your destiny chooses you and your destiny is up to you – only you can make it happen.'

Sami didn't give up. He trained relentlessly, day after day, from sunup till sundown, bound and determined to equal if not surpass the gifted otter. Loki proved a perfect taskmaster, too. Not only was he a great role model and devoted teacher but also a loyal and caring friend who never refused to share his time and expertise for the benefit of his pupil. Sami steadily improved. With infinite satisfaction, he marvelled at the life in his body, at the flair of his performance. When Loki was absent, he'd practice on his own, but when the otter appeared they'd race together at breakneck speed and in perfect unison perform daredevil leaps and rolls that thrilled and dazzled the eyes of the universe. Whenever they performed, predators steered clear; clouds of geese and ducks took to the air and frogs *ribbited* excitedly along the marshy shoreline. During this time of physical growth and self-refinement, Sami's skills improved immensely and so did his size.

Sami's days were so preoccupied with building and fine-tuning his skills that time passed unnoticed. Meanwhile, the eraser of youth was well in hand. Mother Earth had been busy designing him to perfection, carefully rearranging his body towards adulthood, a miracle of anatomical excellence. The once frail and fragile life-form had matured into a strong and fully-grown salmon, ready to venture out and face the great unknown.

Ever since Sami's brief encounter with the white Swan his life had changed dramatically. Schooled and nurtured in the ways of survival, he no longer felt unworthy or ill at ease. Increasingly he sensed the stir of power within, like the flicker of light in a dark world and welcomed its rise like the dawn salutes the sun. With growing confidence, Sami came to think and believe, that given time, he'd pry the secrets from the universe and discover the truth behind his existence.

Eve of Departure

'From innocence to experience'

Springtime and the lake lay flat under an evening sun. Apollo appeared and circled overhead in search of his ward. Sounds of water-play signalled that Sami wasn't far off. Moments later, Sami and Loki arrived, swimming together, side-by-side. Apollo hovered down and settled on the crown of a bulrush stalk, directly overlooking Sami.

'Sami, I bring news concerning you and your destiny,' announced a solemn Apollo. 'Tomorrow, at sunrise, you'll embark on your great journey of self-discovery – a journey designed to take you from innocence to experience – to unlock the mysteries of life – and to open your mind to the truth of your *Self*. It calls for extensive worldwide travel, spanning an indeterminate period of time. You'll pass through distinct and contrasting oceans, venture deep into uncharted waters and discover worlds you never thought existed. You'll visit and explore faraway and unheard-of places – and meet and interact with things unlike anything you've ever seen or known. Undreamed-of wonders wait to delight and confront – each charged with suspense – each offering their own unique challenge. But I urge you, Sami, to exercise care and remain alert, for time and chance happen to everyone. Your journey will be long and full of hazards. There's bound to be days you wished you'd never seen. But bear in mind, Sami, fortune always leaves a door open in times of adversity – every cloud, no matter how dark, is lined with silver. Unfortunately, most of your kind will either stray or lose sight of their goal and fail to measure up to their potential. However, considering your overall fitness along with your discipline and fighting spirit, I see no reason why you cannot live up to and fulfil your destiny.'

Sami viewed his journey with a mixture of high hopes and deep anxiety – for he neither knew his destiny nor the depth of his courage. He wondered, 'will I reach my destination? Will I achieve my destiny? Will I discover the truth behind my existence?' He wanted answers and he needed them now. So, he asked Apollo.

Considerate of Sami's concerns, Apollo took care in constructing his response: 'the unknown will always hold the most fear. But rest assured, Sami, once underway your fears will diminish. As to your destiny, as mentioned before, it is for you alone to bring to light. However, when it comes to courage it's not possible to achieve your destiny without it – and courage can only be discovered, it cannot be taught. Trust and belief in your *Self* is the first step. Then build on that trust – intensify your belief. Risk and uncertainty are part of life, Sami. So be prepared. And if hardship or misfortune should arise, be mindful of the *Self* within – your star of navigation – in other words: *follow the voice of your heart*. Every moment in life, Sami, is a learning experience, a continuous venture into the unknown, and challenges come at you in a thousand different ways. If you're not prepared to confront and overcome, you'll struggle on in vain and never achieve your goal.'

A perfect moon loomed large and bright, coating the lake with a fine luminous film. Apollo continued to counsel and encourage: 'you are greater than you think, Sami. You are beyond measure – bigger than belief. You are destined to be a great beacon of light and inspiration. So, I say to you now – plunge into the unknown – dive deep – go far – and return with confidence, advanced experience and new powers.' Apollo paused to gaze at the purpling sky. 'I see the night has crept upon our talk. Alas, the time has come to bid farewell. You've been given the rare chance to do a special thing – do not lose the opportunity you were born to.' Upon these words, Apollo raised his eyes to the stars, put wings in motion and vanished into the night-time sky.

'So long,' said Sami to a star-studded sky. He wondered if he'd ever see Apollo again. Earlier, Loki had wished him well and then promised they'd meet in the future but now was nowhere in sight. And so, he swam the lake on his own. Moon beams cut sharply through the clear crystal waters. In a melancholy mood, he headed for a pool of light, his mind preoccupied with the upcoming journey. Lost in thought he didn't notice a tiny creature frantically trying to gain attention.

'Hey Sami, slow down!'

Sami turned around and swivelled his eyes. Seeing nothing but empty space he wondered what had caused the commotion. He was sure he'd heard his name called. Then he spied a little spot no bigger than a stone pebble, straining hard to catch him.

'Sami, stop,' it shouted. 'I have a message for you!'

Astonished by such an outburst coming from such a pixie thing, Sami hesitated, warily sizing up the little intruder.

'What do you want?' asked Sami as he contemplated swallowing the plucky noisemaker.

'I know what you're thinking Sami, but don't do it! I can assure you that I am not edible. I bear tidings for your ears only. Pay attention! My name is Maximus and I happen to be a tadpole of high standing.' He then lowered his voice and whispered:

'The key to your destiny lies in the Valley at the bottom of the sea.'

Sami eyed the tadpole with suspicion. Before he could ask for an explanation, the tadpole was gone! *'The key to your destiny lies in the Valley at the bottom of the sea.'* Sami silently repeated the words to himself, committing them to memory. What could they mean? As he searched his mind for clues, a cloud drifted across the face of the moon. Soon the lake was shrouded in darkness. Sami steered towards an enclosure of lake weed and bedded down for the night.

River-Borne and Seabound

'The path grew wide and wider'

A burnished sunrise edged across the lake – a golden pathway, leading to the future. The glory of the sun swept through Sami's heart, filling him with ineffable joy. Lulled by the long, even send of the sea, young and restless salmon abandoned the lake by the thousands, faithful to the lure of the call.

Like an army without harness countless thousands of salmon funnelled through the channel outlet. Lean and swift they yielded freely to the will of the flow. The rising sun poured down unhampered, its probing rays blazing the sea-bound trail. From beneath, against the filtered sun, the salmon glowed in silhouette. Their gilded forms radiated a magnetic charm, a mystic pull compelling to the eye. But one amongst them shone like a rare and precious jewel, one whose bearing held that calm born of determination and one whose heart held that promise worthy of a star.

Sami overflowed with vigour – each nerve sensitive to the slightest change. Eagerly, he slipped into the eye of the current – river-water streaming through his gills – the soft rush pleasing to his ears.

The river unrolled like a magic carpet, unbearably exciting. Crystalline waters hummed a jubilant song – a song victorious that repeated itself over and over again, each note an echo of the first, each note a call to adventure. Propelled by the swift run of the current, the salmon held acceleration in reserve. Enthroned on high, the sun smiled down on kindled spirits and ambitious dreams as childhood memories began to dim and fade away. Sami's doubts and fears dissolved in a parade of dancing water.

The river meandered peacefully in harmony with her bedrock chute. Purling waters wiped the lips of a winding shore, sweeping away the excess debris. On and on, the salmon cruised – on and on the river ran – on and on she shifted the scene. Her endless flow threaded through crowded marshlands – divided lush green forests – slipped smoothly across level plains – split granite mountains – fell freely over headland heights – and skimmed thinly over pans of rock. Her relentless drift adapted to whatever route proved possible but never lost sight of her goal – the river's legendary story to the sea – an ageless struggle to become something greater.

The river possessed an infinite capacity to surprise. She gathered more momentum – swelled with feeding streams – took on more salmon. All at once her genial flow turned strong-minded, striding in long irregular surges. Abruptly she rolled in a drunken gait and started to sprint. Descending more sharply she scrambled noisily over cliffs and plunged spectacularly down canyon walls. Blown to showers, she dissipated into veils of vapour and, evanescing in midair, billowed softly and invisibly in clouds of tinctured mist. Unimpeded, an invigorated Sami enjoyed the thrill of the ride. Then all of a sudden, the river altered her texture to rough and tumble and turned taunting in nature. Cat-like, she toyed with her charge. Yet Sami was impervious to her wild, unruly ways. He excelled in a storm of white-water fury; a free and easy joyride, now dancing this way, now that; at times with a heavy beat, at times with a lightness and grace; an unconstrained spirit in full flight. Life had become a dance and the dance had become him. And the irresistible song of the sea never ceased its seductive call.

So completely did Sami bond with the river that he no longer felt separate from her soul – he *was* the river and as she caressed his silvery sides he joyfully proclaimed: 'You are the river of my heart – the waters of your love feed my soul.'

Sami kept up with his lively play. Like liquid silk he arrowed the surge, all-atingle with expectation. *It's only now that counts*, he thought, and now went along as his constant companion. For one brief, shining moment, Sami became the brightest light in the world.

In high spirits, Sami rode the ever-hastening tide – young, self-assured and strong of body his future never in doubt. Enlivened by his fun filled spree to sea, he gave little thought to anything except letting the moment have its way. Meanwhile, unbeknownst to Sami, an invisible thread finely spun from celestial imagination, trailed unwaveringly in his wake.

Physical Change

'A shock to the system'

Further downriver, a hunting party of long-legged heron waded stealthily into the shallow shore. The salmon carried on, unmindful of impending disaster. Suddenly, like a thunderclap, the intoxicating peace was shattered! Without warning, a whirlwind of darting heads and snapping beaks incited panic and mass confusion. Sami dashed for deeper waters. But as he reached the safety of mid-channel depths, squadrons of merganser ducks launched separate attacks. These flying predators had the ability to dive deep beneath the surface and perform like fish. They presented a far greater challenge.

With strong, rapid kicks, Sami surged ahead. Wheeling obliquely like a fighter plane he narrowly averted the diving ducks. Most of his companions followed his lead. Fortunately, the ducks were slow and clumsy and constantly had to resurface for air. After a harrowing stretch of dodging beaks and clutching claws, the winged hunters were left behind.

On the following sunrise, the dawning light silvered the river, giving hints of a trouble-free day. Meanwhile, the shorelines moved further apart – the current lost its momentum – the depths became less shallow. The salmon were on the edge of a new and powerful world. Then all at once when least expected, a stunning jolt threw them in disarray. The river had drastically altered her texture, restricting their ability to breathe. The shock was sharp and fierce, causing a painful, suffocating sensation, which threatened to turn them back. As the first bitter strains filtered through Sami's gills, he faltered and lost control. No longer was he in familiar waters but in unknown territory, a world devoid of freshwater – a world that forced him to adapt or perish.

Initially the briny water was painful to take in, as if a toxic drug. Its paralyzing effect caused the salmon to languish and flounder, sending them dangerously close to the surface. They soon became comatose, making easy prey for diving birds and plunging ducks. A blitzkrieg of vicious air attacks followed. Swarms of herons, terns and razor-beaked hawks attacked at will. The birds dived and plunged, then clawed their way back into the sky, cramming down their catch. The feeding frenzy went on and on and on …

Like most of his kind, Sami drifted unresistingly, powerless, almost belly-up. The saltwater had rendered him insensible. High in the sky a silver bird witnessed the carnage raging below and focused on one victim only. Abruptly, the bird banked its flight, swept its wings and streaked down to the stricken Sami, skidding to a stop by his side. In a voice loud and clear the bird commanded, 'BREATHE DEEP – DIVE DEEP!' Sami listened and reacted. He opened his gills, drew in the briny water, then painstakingly forced his body downwards, down into deeper, safer depths. In short order, his strength returned like an incoming tide. The energy infused renewed his resolve. With strong, aggressive kicks, Sami was on his way.

Sami had undergone a physical transformation, making a transition from freshwater to saltwater. In a short while, the shorelines drifted further and further apart and soon disappeared altogether. The river had slowed to a crawl, her yearning stilled, her coppery hue exchanged for bluish green. After a hard and punishing drive, the river had run her course, fulfilled her quest and finally become one with the sea. Her life had ended in order to be part of something greater – a vast and powerful ocean.

With mission accomplished, the river surrendered the salmon to the sea. Clouds of shorebirds circled overhead, shocking the air with piercing, high-pitched shrills – their predatory eyes tracking the migrating fish. Like a wash of silver, the salmon streamed into the sea. The birds focused on stragglers only. Sami slipped by unnoticed. He'd met the world he was destined to join. And each sweep of his tail drove him further from home but closer to truth.

The Ocean

'A new and powerful world'

The ocean beat like a separate heart, a will all its own. Sami entered its enormity with excited expectation. The slow cadence of tidal breathing aroused his curiosity, but not his fear. Once engaged with its wide-open reach there would be no turning back. Its endless shift – its constant push and pull sent a perpetual and inviting echo.

Sami had gained access to a world of high adventure and unprecedented danger. Before him lay vast solitudes and beyond these even vaster solitudes, an immensity of ocean wilderness. As he advanced further and deeper into its silence, he proceeded with a mixture of caution and confidence. His destiny, as always, occupied a place in his mind, but for now his thoughts were centred on the journey only.

To the uninitiated the ocean gave an extraordinary sense of space and distance – a stretching infinity to everywhere and nowhere. Undaunted, Sami steered a steady, unvarying course, content to go along with his companions. Predictably, as he adapted to ocean living, his anxiety became tempered with a growing sense of self-reliance.

Swift 'neath the waves with finned speed they flew – untroubled minds in a sea of hopeful dreams. Sami enjoyed a freedom never known before. Attaining perfect unity, boundless thousands moved as one, league upon league, day after day – a glittering sphere of silver, venturing into a strange and wondrous universe. The voyage unfolded uneventfully – endless miles unwound – expectations ran high – Sami's destination – still a mist.

Absorbed in its silent awareness the ocean proved indifferent to all that tread her boundaries. For Sami, day-to-day survival was not unlike his native waters, where tension ran high and life expectancy – a known uncertainty. He could never relax. As always, he must be on constant alert, avoid predators and forage for food. In the beginning, he felt the loss of Apollo, and sorely missed his counsel. But as the journey lengthened, the stream, the lake and former friends slipped further and further into obscurity.

The salmon travelled the subsurface currents that circled round the planet. These strong-moving flows enabled them to cover great distance with relative ease. Progress was good. Instinct ruled as the sun does the earth, but for Sami it was different. Frequently, he'd spearhead the others in attempts to find the elusive key to his destiny. But his efforts were for naught and his destination remained, as always, shrouded in secrecy. Even though disappointed, Sami continued to gain in experience. Each day created a new world, friends made – enemies established. It was a theme he'd grown used to, complete with all its twists and turns.

One day, the ocean-grey gave way to mint-green. The salmon had entered a patch of sea unusually rich in plant life. Everywhere, leafy strands of plankton patterned the surface, ribbons of seaweed meandered at will while in deeper depths, swales of sea grass swayed gently with the evening flow. As the sun sank lower, the sea turned into darker shades of twilight and shadow. Abandoned on the ocean floor, the ghostly remains of a surface vessel looked oddly out of place. Upright and stripped of sail, its barren masts teetered on the verge of collapse. After a lingering glance, Sami curbed his curiosity and bypassed the ship for a meal of kelp. Hidden in the background, sharp eyes tracked his every move. A sense of foreboding kept rising in Sami's mind. Ignoring the omen, he continued to feed.

Dark titanic shapes circled round and around in ever-narrowing rings. Shadowy figures loomed, appeared distorted, humped and alien. From the confusion of shadows, a darker one detached itself and moved forward unhurriedly, yet deliberately. It was Mordred, an enormous rogue shark, thirsting for blood. From the corner of his eye, Sami caught the shark moving as silent as thought towards his companions – its mouth a gaping funnel of teeth. A train of possibilities raced through his mind – his schooling nature drew him towards his comrades – self-preservation urging flight. Stricken by fear he froze, powerless to act. With savage, cold-blooded precision, the shark lunged at its prey. Gripped by the dread of extinction the salmon made frantic efforts to flee. Sami recoiled in horror as powerful jaws ripped, shredded and swallowed his companions. Craving more, the shark wheeled around and locked its eyes on Sami, devouring him in its gaze. A blade of panic sliced through his heart. Programmed to kill, the shark moved in a rigid mode of locate, attack and destroy. Sami stared wild-eyed, petrified. The efficient executioner with its evil-looking grin was fully primed and set to strike. As it closed for the kill its monstrous head grew massive in size – its cold lifeless eyes flared into hatred – its yawning cavernous jaws boasted sharp, pinnacle teeth. To Sami's horror they all pointed one way, to a deep black hole.

The shark lunged at Sami. Then unexpectedly swerved away, staggering in stunned confusion. Shocked and threatened anger took command. Its mood ugly it stormed after Sami. And once again was denied when a phantom fist cannoned into its gut. In obvious pain, the shark withdrew, retreating into the darkness below. Moments later, a pearl-grey sea mammal appeared. Its size dwarfed the frightened Sami, but its gentle eyes signalled a friend.

'Don't be alarmed, Sami. You have a friend in me,' assured a pleasant voice.

'My name is Juno. I appear as a dolphin,' she kindly informed him.

'Rest easy – Mordred won't be claiming any more victims today. Gather your comrades and follow me.'

A tense yet relieved Sami located a few of his kind. With ranks badly depleted, the survivors trailed behind the dolphin. Death and disaster never ceased to take its toll. Ocean living proved no different than inland waters where loss of life was frequent and commonplace. To Sami it seemed like nothing had changed except the scenery.

The dolphin led the wary salmon through the shark-infested waters. The sharks scattered in pursuit of easier prey. Like a good shepherd, Juno kept a watchful eye, paying close attention to Sami. Once clear of danger, she drew him aside and gently jogged his memory, 'Count yourself lucky this time Sami, but in future listen to the *Self* within – the voice of your heart.'

Still shaken, Sami simply nodded. He felt an odd mixture of excitement and relief. Thanks to Juno he'd stared death in the face and lived to see another day. Yet he also knew that if it hadn't been for her timely intervention, he no longer would exist. In any case, all he wanted now was to get on with his journey and leave these treacherous waters behind.

'Not to worry, Sami, we all live in eternity,' said Juno. 'Loosen up – relax – tomorrow is another day. When good fortune comes your way – be thankful and consider it a blessing. And Sami, need I remind you,

'The key to your destiny lies in the Valley at the bottom of the sea.'

Startled, Sami exclaimed, 'The tadpole, Maximus, whispered those words to me – but then vanished without saying what they meant.'

'Be patient, Sami. You'll soon find out,' said Juno. Then she promptly waved her tail and veered into invisibility.

'The tadpole's message must be important,' reasoned Sami.

'It must hold a hidden meaning. Otherwise, it wouldn't have been delivered twice.'

Deep in thought, he hurried off to join his companions, racking his brain, trying to unriddle the riddle.

Lost and abandoned, the salmon resumed their journey – a lonely clutch of fish deep in the middle of nowhere.

The Storm

'The depths of the sea are calm'

A new day dawned, yet the sun failed to rise. The troubled sea hugely heaved and turned darker than dark. Fear and tension rode the waves. Anger climbed with each whip of the elements. Bolts of flame seared the heavens and the heavens struck back with deafening roars. All at once the full pent-up might of an ocean storm let loose with all its fury. Fuelled by the bottommost depths of the sea the surface abruptly erupted and exploded in cataclysmic upheaval. Howling gales intensified and grew merciless. Waves raced in terror, their thrashing crests white with foam. Rolling swells gained magnitude, surged upwards and soared into huge, towering monsters. Directed by a power beyond comprehension great volumes of sea were resurrected from the deeps and hurled along in liquid mountains as dire and ruthless as a screaming avalanche.

Sami reeled out of control, caught in the mad eye of an ocean storm, a cyclonic blowout that respected no laws or dimensions. The explosive motion of the ocean, its horrendous, whirl-away upsurge threatened to harm and destroy him altogether. From skyline-to-skyline waves mounted higher and higher, building up to staggering heights.

Soaring with the peaks, plunging with the troughs, Sami was the toy of wind and waves, tossed and flung about with shocking violence. He felt exposed and vulnerable. A voice kept repeating, '*The depths of the sea are calm no matter how wild and stormy the top – let go of the wave, be one with the sea.*' Sami listened – and understood. He angled his fins, kicked his tail and headed down to the ocean floor. Down – down and down he dived – ever lower ever deeper. The light dissolved, turning from pale to grey to dark to nothing at all. Sami kept kicking, descending to a level where few had ever been.

As Sami intruded the iron dark spaces, imagined terrors fuelled his burgeoning fears. Deprived of sight and sense of direction, he soon became lost and disorientated. All at once a swirling undertow swept up and grabbed hold. Its siphoning action spun him down still deeper. Driven by fear he fought a desperate battle to reverse his course but with gathering speed he kept spinning horribly downwards. The impact was terrifying, taking Sami where nothing could protect him. He went beyond the deep of deeps, swamped down into a black bottomless hole. In panic he decided, as a last resort, to relinquish his grip and surrender all resistance. By so doing, he gave way to a force so great and powerful that he suddenly breached the wall of the unknown. He strained his eyes in the pitch-black dark. It seemed to Sami that he'd reached a place where even the sun feared to tread.

Sami's senses groped amidst the velvet black. The dark soaked up all sound. He could neither see nor hear. Utter stillness prevailed, only made more eerie for what had gone before. He made no move that could attract attention. He felt as if he were frozen in time, suspended between worlds, adrift in an endless, lightless void. The absolute stillness made him uneasy but strangely receptive. Before long, even the darkness appeared to move, as if breaking into hundreds of hungry creatures.

The Valley

Piercing the dark an angel of light,
A starry vision burning bright,
Rays of gold from golden throne,
Softly, softly, open the night,
And call to a place unknown.

And then something extraordinary happened! A light began to tear a tiny hole in the dark. A glimmer of hope! Where did it come from? It seemed to be trapped in the dark just like Sami. It flickered momentarily then blazed into brightness. Sami froze in the unexpected glare. The inky blackness retreated. A shimmering dome of light surrounded him. He felt a curious and disturbing sense of awe and did not know why but was absorbed by its splendour. A delicate, crystalline orb pulsed into view, revealing a wraithlike corona of silver-white light. From its core, there began a steady palpitating, pure and majestic, like wings of light, endless multitudes of them, which spread broadly and vastly, banishing the all-consuming dark. The spectacle radiated in unparalleled brilliance. Points of light circled its presence like celestial stars. The dark dissolved, the present slipped out of focus and Sami dwelled in the realms of magic. A surrealistic seascape began to shape itself out of the dark. It was as if a condensed drop of light had dropped into the sea and the light had spread, and the outlines of an inviting dream had rippled into bright relief.

A voice of infinite kindness broke the silence, washing through Sami as gently as a wave of music. ‘What you are searching for, Sami, is also searching for you – welcome – welcome to the Valley of Awareness and Forgetfulness.’ The greeting echoed softly from the source of light.

In a voice barely audible, Sami stammered, ‘w-w-who are you? W-w-where am I?’

‘I am the bringer of the brightest light of all – the Light of Truth,’ came the reply.

‘I am the Angel of Light – the liberator of souls. In your eyes I appear as a moon jellyfish. My name is Venus. My role is to point you to the truth of your *Self.*’

Dumbstruck with wonder, Sami stared in blank astonishment.

‘Out of the abyss I have called unto thee and you have heard my call,’ said the Angel.

‘You would not have sought me had you not already found me. I’ve been with you since the beginning of the beginning. During your long existence there have been times when you thought life to be empty and meaningless and yet, deep down, you knew there must be more than what met the eye. Did you think your mind or imagination made you hear a different tune? It was the call of *Self,* begging you to come home.’

Sami looked bewildered, his mind in turmoil. What, he wondered, did the Angel mean by long existence?

Venus proceeded to address Sami’s thoughts: ‘Never have I not existed – nor have you – and never shall we cease to exist. Birth and death are only a game of hide and seek. Does the wind die when it ceases to blow? Are the waves dead when the sea is calm? Is a cloud no more when it turns into rain? Only the physical form is destructible – never the Life Source. The Valley of Awareness and Forgetfulness is a safety zone or haven, free of earthly cares and fears – a sanctuary of peace and endless awakenings where time disappears and the unknown begins. The Valley is where hope is renewed, and despair denied – where doubt is cast aside, and you simply *Know* – it's where you discover your innermost *Self.* Forget the past and open your mind to love and truth – recognize the goodness that abides within you. In the Valley, you are never unloved and there is nothing you can do wrong. Let go of your fears – believe in your *Self* – aim high and soar!'

Sami listened, spellbound, unable to speak.

'You've come to the Valley as a broken dream – a god in ruins. The door of awareness is unlocked – enter and open your mind – may it be filled with light.'

When Sami found his voice, he gathered his courage and asked, 'Why am I the only one? Where are the others – my companions?'

Venus spoke slowly, pausing from time to time to allow Sami to keep pace and understand: 'Sami, it's not chance that brought you to the Valley. You are here because you are one whose heart is more directed to its destiny. For that reason, alone, you shall be enlightened and empowered with the timeless truths of the universe – a gift bestowed on few – and given freely with unconditional love. The longing for truth runs deep in your soul. Over many lifetimes you have struggled long and hard in search of it. Yet truth is an elusive quarry and even when found is difficult to grasp. Once revealed, however, it gives you the freedom to turn away from the forces of dark and evil and turn to the forces of light and love. You're in the greatest depths of despair when you don't know who you are. The greatest fulfilment of existence is to discover who you are. *And the greatest sensation of all is not to trust but to know.'*

To Sami this sounded too good to be true. He half-wondered if he was dreaming a dream or caught in a weird and make-believe fantasy. Then again, he thought, *perhaps the Valley is my destination!* But overly cautious and lacking in confidence he hesitated to ask.

Venus continued to elaborate and enlighten: 'Truth is like a long-lost pearl in the ocean and few there are who find it. We misuse Truth when we give it to those who are not yet ready – it is not given lightly. Truth will lift you out of the dark and into the light – Truth will open the windows of your eyes and unlock the doors of your mind – Truth will give your soul the freedom to sing and dance, to praise and love – *Truth shall set you free.* Open your mind to the illogical – be receptive to what is unconceived, unimagined, unexpected, unnamed. Discover what is boundless – discover the power behind the universe – discover the limitless *Self*!'

Sami's eyes glazed over, awash in confusion, alive with questions!

'When your visit comes to an end and you resume your journey, you'll start from the same place you were at before you entered the Valley. On your journey home, you'll forget most, if not all, of your entire Valley experience. Nevertheless, truth is permanent and unfading and once revealed cannot be unlearned. It becomes part of you and stays with you for now and forevermore. Know that the best is yet to be – the present better than the past – and the future better than the present, because you never stop learning – and never do you stop advancing. So, I say to you now, know what has always been and greet the unknown with confidence. Celebrate the vastness of being – rejoice in the grand adventure.'

The dark misgivings of the past lifted from Sami's mind like a fleet of bad dreams. The Valley's all-around serenity, its magnetic charm and overwhelming appeal prompted Sami to accept and believe that his searching was over – that he'd achieved his goal. But unsure of his feelings and being overly cautious he chose to say nothing and remain silent. *There's no point in asking*, he thought, *and being let down and disappointed.* So, he decided to ask the deepest and most profound question of all: 'What is the purpose of life?'

'The purpose of life,' replied Venus, 'is to discover your *Self.*'

In a magical way, Sami had crossed into a wonderland of rarefied beauty, empty of suffering, free of strife, altogether detached from the world he knew. His eyes danced with delight as they skipped over a wealth of undisguised temptations, each defying belief, each waiting to be discovered. The Valley's unspoiled perfection, its unbroken wholeness and irresistible appeal presented an ethereal otherworldliness, a dream within a dream where the senses are overpowered and the real and unreal become delightfully tangled. A perennial serenity reigned over all. Sami could not contain his joy. He convinced himself that he'd unriddled the riddle – that he'd found the key to his destiny.

The Valley celebrated the arrival of Sami with great joy and fanfare. Vivid rainbows arched overhead, bands of light fanned out like luminous wands and flamboyant wonders materialized out of nowhere. But most captivating and indeed impressive, under a canopy of cobalt-blue, orbiting moons and streaking comets merged with light-pulsing stars of emerald, sapphire, ruby and diamond, bedazzling the Valley with a vibrant spectrum of colour. The electrifying demonstration cast a spell of magic. Sami wished the euphoria would never end, the sensation of being completely and spectacularly alive. A surging spring of excitement mingled with sheer unalloyed joy made Sami triumphantly declare, 'At last I've found my destination!'

No sooner had Sami claimed victory than a little seahorse popped into view. Elegant, bright-eyed, and hardly bigger than a shrimp, the elfin stallion displayed a proud equine head topped off with a tiny golden crown. He radiated a regal yet jovial air. Sami couldn't help but admire his buoyant nature. The seahorse pranced and danced before the fascinated Sami, anxious to show off the grandeur of the Valley.

'My name is Pegasus,' he cheerfully announced.

'It is my great pleasure, indeed, my distinct honour, to escort you through the Valley.'

And with a flare of his nostrils and a flick of his tail, he charged off shouting, 'Tally Ho! Follow me!'

Rapt in wonder and too stunned to ask if he'd found the key to his destiny, Sami respectfully followed the seahorse. He was curious as to what Venus had meant when she said, 'one day he would leave the Valley and return home.' But why would he want to leave? As far as he was concerned the Valley was home. He planned to stay forever. Moments later, however, while trailing behind the seahorse, he was struck by an odd feeling – a bizarre feeling of being disconnected, a stranger in a nowhere world, lost in a weird and wonderful dream.

With special care and attention to detail the seahorse introduced Sami to his new surroundings. To Pegasus it was like showing the Valley to a foreign entity, an intelligent, thoughtful individual whose eyes surveyed the sights with pleasure, often with delight, but one who appeared to be looking beyond them, attempting to reconcile each new attraction with the world from which he came. For his part, Sami was a stranger, anxious not to draw attention by any wrong move or breach of manners. But in spite of his best efforts to do so he could not conceal his sense of wonderment – everything that met his eye possessed itself of great novelty.

Sami now found himself on the receiving end of a natural outpouring of love and nurturing. His life had taken a complete turn, placing him in a world supernaturally free of the insecurities of the past. In some fortuitous way, he'd been liberated and delivered to an irresistible land of enchantment, no longer connected to the fine threads of chance and circumstance.

As the tour neared its end, Sami and Pegasus came upon a five-pointed star, lying motionless on the ocean floor. The star didn't budge from its sandy bed but lay like a stationary sentinel, indifferent to all.

'This is Odin,' introduced Pegasus. 'He is an Asteroidean, better known as a Starfish. Odin is an intellectual mastermind – a virtual wellspring of information. If you need to know anything about anything, all you need to do is ask Odin.'

As Sami nosed in for a closer look, the starfish unexpectedly spoke. 'The key that you seek cannot to be found in the Valley – neither can it be found across the ocean-sea. It can only be found in your heart.'

This remark took Sami by surprise. He had yet to ask anyone about the *key* for he desperately wanted to believe that the Valley was the *key*. He then grew curious as to how the Starfish could know his name or, incredibly, what was on his mind?

'Allow me to explain,' said Pegasus. 'In the Valley thoughts have a higher dwelling place than in the physical world. Whenever you think you give birth to your thoughts. Whatever the mind can conceive and believe, the mind can achieve. The possibilities are endless. You're limited only by your imagination. After all, the power of thought created the universe. It's really quite simple – no sooner thought than done. All you need is a little practice.'

The idea of turning invisible thought into visible form thoroughly fascinated Sami. He decided to give it a try. With studied concentration, he focused his mind on his favourite food. As if by magic, a banquet of luscious plankton appeared, their green shoots just ripe for consumption. While nibbling away on the leafy stems, he fixed his mind on a meal of kelp. Without delay, the savoury delicacy carpeted the seafloor. *Here I am*, thought Sami, *in an endless paradise, gorging myself to my heart's delight. Surely, I must be dreaming!*

Pegasus, looking on nearby, smiled to himself and said: 'The world goes round and round in make believe, Sami. It's all a dream within a dream. Though most are unaware, we are all but transitory guests visiting this planet called Earth. Recognize that everything is spirit – there is no death – there is only continuation. So never take life too seriously. It's simply an adventure – a grand illusion. If you attach too much importance to the ups and downs of life, it becomes a burden, causing anxiety and discontent. So never be afraid to take a chance. One who is overcautious will accomplish little. When you open yourself to new possibilities, you never know what you can achieve. Know that tomorrow never comes – there is only the present. Yesterday is consumed by today and today exists only to bring forth tomorrow.' After a brief pause, Pegasus asked: 'Do you wish to know more, Sami – shall I continue?'

Since Sami possessed a fertile and inquiring mind he eagerly replied, 'Please, go on!'

The seahorse shed further light: 'Thoughts are like links in a chain that binds you to your fellow beings. In the Valley our natural means of communication is through thought. You see what lies behind appearance – know that you are not merely a physical form. Imagine a life with absolute freedom – a life with no horizons – a life free of pain and suffering – a life that time can never conquer.' Sami's interest piqued sharply when Pegasus next revealed; 'I have the means to see into the future – to predict things that ordinarily are unpredictable.'

While Sami weighed the merits of this claim, Pegasus announced, 'It's time to visit the Forest of Enchantment and discover the hidden secrets of the Crystal Mountain!'

In friendly fashion, Pegasus and Sami hurried off to visit the Mountain. The seahorse chose a fascinating yet roundabout route that took them through dark mysterious caves, through intricate coral networks and through deep romantic canyons. They passed the time in idle conversation, enjoying the sights along the way. Sami marvelled at the diversity of the seascape – its ever-changing and creative nature. As they swam side-by-side Sami let his imagination run loose. After a while, seemingly out of nowhere, what he was imagining burst into existence. Sami gaped in wonder. The scene before him portrayed a breath-taking, eye-filling spectacular, a wish-fulfilling fantasy where reality failed to cooperate. Far exceeding his expectations, the scene that filled his eyes teemed with tall, overhanging trees, profusions of soft, feathery foliage, and endless varieties of flowering plants. But most striking and far beyond what language could describe the entirety of it all was frozen in bright, glittering crystal. The whole forest simply pulsated with lights. Countless lights skipped, hopped, winked, and blinked. The overall effect so mesmerized and distracted Sami that he almost lost sight of Pegasus. As they proceeded further and deeper into the forest, Sami's curiosity grew even more intense. All at once, a rising slipstream propelled him up and over the treetops where, to his surprise and amazement, a wondrous sight dazzled his eyes. Soaring majestically from the ocean floor radiated a radiance that rivalled the sun – immensely and violently brilliant the Crystal Mountain towered before him in all its magnificence. Solid and transparent, its multifaceted surface formed infinite numbers of angles, each one a separate prism. They attracted and refracted light, showering the seascape with a continuous play of colour. Pegasus circled round and selected one of the prisms. After signalling for Sami to follow, he disappeared through a haze of light. Sami stayed close behind. They'd both gained access to a long narrow tunnel, a secret passageway. Like a distant mirage, a separate image of Sami and Pegasus glimmered at the far end. Together they proceeded towards the two figures. As Sami drew near, he began to fade and flow into his own image. Suddenly, as if struck by lightning, he was conscious of a different awareness. Somehow, he'd entered a parallel universe – a world living in a future dimension of time.

It wasn't long before Sami sensed a tension build, a feeling of unease. The brilliant colours dissolved into sinister shades of grey. Strange effects began to accrue out of the semi-darkness. Fragmented bones, scoured and half-buried, lay scattered on the ocean floor. Shadows opened into shadows and everything appeared frozen in a murky, eerie glow. An uneasy silence prevailed. Deeper down and barely visible, an ill-fated ship languished on its own, its ribs exposed like a ravaged skeleton. Glassy bubbles wept from its open portholes. Three encrusted masts, sea-worn and draped with drift-weed, tilted at awkward angles. A curious fish of the salmon species attracted notice as it lingered behind to inspect the fallen ship. As if sensing another's presence the curious salmon abruptly turned and stared straight at Sami, its eyes blank, registering nothing. Sami recognized one of his kind – he was looking directly at himself! Shivers tingled up his spine.

'I brought you here to give you a glimpse of the future,' said Pegasus, 'to show you things that have not yet happened but will happen. Your eyes bear witness to a moment in the future, looming in the distance. The vision projected portrays an event that concerns you and your destiny. It takes place in the physical world – the world from which you came – and therefore not governed by our laws. But be warned, Sami, avoid all ships, whether above or below the surface. The most menacing are ships that float on the surface and are recognized by their prolonged roars. Also avoid ships that settle on the bottom of the sea as they give cover to hungry predators. Always steer clear and keep your distance – don't let curiosity get the best of you – don't be tempted into something you cannot undo!'

As the scene played out, a massive rogue shark emerged from the ship's hold. Mordred, the bringer of death, was on the prowl, thirsting for blood. With cunning stealth, he circled round the ship, approaching Sami's image from behind. Abruptly, without warning, his jaws gaped open and swallowed it whole!

Shaken by what the future revealed, Sami vowed he'd never go near ships again and he'd always keep his distance. He recalled the dolphin, Juno, and how Mordred had almost ended his days. Sami had no intention of trading the comforts and safety of the Valley for the dangers and hardships of his former world. He was quite content with his current lifestyle and said as much to Pegasus. The seahorse solemnly acknowledged Sami's promise. And so, without delay, the two returned to the present time and the sanctuary of the Valley.

Sami's journey of *Self*-discovery inevitably moved across the stage of time. He came to be one of the most popular mortals in the Valley. Frequently, his mind was overloaded with strange and profound ideas. At times, it seemed the more he knew the less he understood. Nevertheless, he appreciated the kindness and generosity extended to him. However, even though his dreams never failed to come true and, as a result, he could have and do anything he pleased, life seemed to pass in slow successions of nothing. The Valley's lack of danger, its overall safeness and never-ending peace had at first filled his heart with tranquillity and joy. But as time went by, he became haunted by a gnawing restlessness, a sense of something unfulfilled. It was a weird sensation, a vague feeling of emptiness and frustration, which he could neither explain nor justify – and however hard he tried he could not escape the intensity of its nagging. The Valley had lulled him into complacency, a false sense of security, and now he seemed to be marking time, waiting for his future to start. Sami thought he had everything he could possibly desire, but he also felt there must be more. And, as so often the case, whatever was missing refused to give him peace. Therefore, on a sudden impulse he decided to visit Odin, the all-knowing starfish, to seek his counsel.

'Look within to find what you seek,' advised the wise Odin. 'The paradox of comfort is that you stop trying. Without adversity, without change, life becomes meaningless. Life is a journey to discover who you are. You may think you know but Sami, you have no idea. The single most important work you can be engaged in is to discover and know your *Self*. That's why you were brought to the Valley – to open your mind and gain *Self-awareness*. Your intellect has yet to have all the answers. Nevertheless, they are rooted deep within your *Self* and it's only a matter of time before they surface and wake you to the truth. From the first moment, you arrived you've been busy rebuilding, reshaping, reconfiguring, adjusting. Realize that enlightenment has only a beginning and no end.' After a short pause, Odin asked, 'Does this help you, Sami? Do you understand?'

'Yes, I believe so. At least I think I do. Thank you,' said Sami, respectfully. Then out of curiosity he asked, 'What does intellect mean?'

'It's some sort of tool or device you have in your mind,' explained Odin.

'It allows you to remember things and lets you shuffle them around so you can figure them out.'

'Oh – I see,' nodded Sami, thoughtfully.

The tortoise, Merlin, listening in nearby, poked his wizened head out of his prominent humped-back shell and addressed Sami: 'The uncertainty of life is its seduction. The Valley offers no such uncertainty, no challenge or obstacles to overcome, nothing to accomplish, neither triumphs nor failures. Time weighs heavy when it's empty with no goal or purpose to fill its gap. In your world, Sami, any task, regardless of size, requires effort. In the Valley, it's just the opposite. Here you fly high on borrowed wings. Everything comes too easy. It's different for us. We've met and overcome the trials and tribulations of the Earth World and now our purpose is to aid and comfort those who haven't.'

'There's something wonderful stirring deep within you that's doing its best to flower,' revealed Odin. 'And you know this to be true, Sami. You're on the verge of discovering your *Self.* Can you not sense the tremors of change – the import of the occasion – the magnitude of the event?'

'Yes, I do feel somewhat strange,' admitted Sami. 'But it's hard to explain. My feelings don't seem to lend themselves to words.'

'Never mind, Sami, in time they will,' encouraged Odin. And in his infinite wisdom the starfish proceeded to share his knowledge: 'Life in your world has many 'ifs and the threads that weave the pattern of your existence appear so haphazard that you're inclined to attribute to chance what should be put down to fate. What appears the merest accident springs from the deepest source of destiny. Your visit to the Valley is by no means an accident or misadventure. It was prearranged long ago and designed to help you find your *Self* and thus prepare you for your destination.'

'What are you saying?' cried Sami. 'That the Valley is not my destination – not my home!'

'Indeed, it is not,' replied Odin. 'Something far more glorious awaits you at journeys end. Seek and you shall find!'

Sami could not hold back his disappointment. 'How will I know what I'm looking for, when I don't know where or what it is? If I don't know where it is then how will I know where I'm going and why?' said Sami, exasperated. 'Sometimes I don't know what I do know even though I know what I know is knowable, and yet I cannot know the unknowable – if I could it would be knowable. As for what is or is not knowable, I don't know that I know.'

A shimmer of light signalled the arrival of Venus. Her angelic presence bathed the gathering in a soft luminous glow.

'Please let me explain,' said Venus.

'Truth is not meant to crush but to elevate. Our aim is to dismantle presumptions, defamiliarize the familiar and render the incomprehensible comprehensible. The Valley is an out-of-the-world retreat where you can break free from the past, unburden your burdens and discover the core of your being. Before you came to the Valley you were aware of only your outer you and not your inner you or your *Self*. And your *Self* is crying out to be discovered. Once discovered it filters into your heart like a welcoming light. It grows in you and speaks to you. All you have to do is listen.'

Venus then went on to let Sami know that his Valley visit had served its purpose and was drawing to a close. 'Soon you'll be on your way,' she said.

'But before you go, you will know your destiny and why it is so important.'

Noting Sami's confusion, Venus explained: 'The forces of light and dark are in constant struggle. The inner you is a battlefield between these two. Acts of evil allows dark to bend its way. Acts of kindness level the scales. When light and dark have equal play, the former is always an overmatch for the latter.'

Venus paused momentarily before she revealed Sami's destiny: 'Today, planet Earth is drowning in darkness and in desperate need of help,' said Venus.

'Your destiny, Sami, is to bear the darkness of the World and transform it into light.'

Sami mulled this over for a long time until curiosity forced him to ask, 'How is it possible to turn dark into light – to make the impossible possible?'

'There is no darkness that the light of *Self* cannot penetrate,' replied Venus.

'But before you turn dark into light you must first find the key!'

'But I thought I'd found the key when I found the Valley!' exclaimed Sami.

'No,' said Venus. 'You have yet to find the key!'

'Why is the key so important?' pressed Sami.

'The key opens the door to *Self-awareness* and without *Self-awareness* you cannot fulfil your destiny!'

'In plain language, please explain what you mean?' pleaded Sami.

'Life, Sami, is a constant struggle to discover and know your *Self* and then to allow your *Self* to lead you safely home. To keep from erring along the way requires courage. But to have courage you must know your *Self.* And only you can know your *Self* and only *Self* can give you courage. It's both simple and complicated – but your destiny demands it.'

Sami tried to make sense out of this senseless explanation. It sounded simple enough and yet he couldn't seem to grasp it. Flustered and mentally stymied he once more appealed to Venus. 'Please Venus, spell out exactly what you mean – please disentangle, unravel, untwist, unknot, unscramble – but tell me something – tell me anything that lets me know what you mean – that I can understand!'

After this display of frustration Sami's mind settled into deep thought. After a short while, he posed the question whose answer had long eluded him: 'What is the Truth behind my existence?'

For a long time, Venus remained silent and then in a quiet unhurried way she lifted the veil of secrecy. Carefully she pronounced each of her carefully chosen words: 'All of creation from the tiny sand granule to the shining star in the sky is connected like links in a chain. The truth behind your existence is immutable and indestructible. The life you think of as your own has existed throughout the ages for eons upon eons with uninterrupted progression. Your life-stream is like a mountain river – it springs from unseen sources – is of earthly origin – is linked to the stars – transmutes – migrates – evolves. You are a guardian of the life-stream – a temporary expression of a far greater being and destined to return to its source. Sami, you are truth itself – a beautiful child of the universe.'

The tone and rhythm of her voice combined to lull Sami into a deep, dream-laden sleep. In a stunning revelation, he saw what was not possible to see in a conscious state and over the course of his dreaming the secrets of the universe passed from Venus to Sami. Upon completion, Sami accepted without apprehension the totality of his existence and celebrated the vastness of being.

'Psssst … Sami, are you awake?'

Sami's eyes focused on three limbs, waving like whips cracking in slow motion. He recognized the octopus, Pluto, 'Mmm … yes … I think so,' he murmured, drowsily.

'Truth is a deep kindness,' said Pluto, 'It teaches us to be content with our everyday life and to share with our neighbour the same happiness. Know also how luck plays a role in the drama of life and how little we have to worry about anything except doing our best.'

Before he took leave, Pluto casually mentioned, 'See you later, Sami, at a different place – and a different time,' whereupon, he inhaled deeply, levitated slightly, and with a sudden swoosh, propelled into disappearance.

A voice from the distant past transported Sami on memory's wings to a far-off mountain stream. 'The day that you linger is the day you lose forever. Come home Sami, come home – come back to where you belong.'

'Is that you, Apollo?' cried an overjoyed Sami. 'Is that you that stands so close to my heart, yet unseen by my eyes?'

'Yes, Sami, it is me, Apollo, your friend and guide,' said the voice. 'The restless feeling that disturbs you so is your inner longing. Longing is your great ally, Sami. It is the call of *Self,* begging you to come home!'

Visions of home raced through Sami's mind, stirring memories of a long-forgotten stream.

'Each moment presents a choice that can change the story of your life,' said Apollo. 'Home is where you belong, Sami – home is where fear and sorrow cannot exist. Choose wisely, Sami – come back to where you're meant to be.'

A great stabbing loneliness gripped Sami. He felt its emptiness like an abyss between his heart and the heart of his longing.

'Our struggle is over,' said Pegasus.

'But your struggle is still in progress. Our purpose is to guide and steer you through life's incredible maze. We will never abandon you. Wherever you are, we will be there too. Your happiness is our happiness. On your homeward journey, every enlightened soul on every plane throughout the universe will remind, support, push, pull, cheer, embrace; do whatever is needed to see you safely home. For we are called to your side because you are called to the truth of your *Self.*'

'*Self-belief* draws down the powers of the universe,' said Venus. 'Learn to harness that power – to moderate it – to make it work for you. It is your lifeline Sami, a tether that will never break – the silver cord that will lead you home. You have a great role to play. Stop waiting for the future. The future is here, now. Your time has come to shine.'

For Sami, the Valley had been a great blessing – a time of truth – a time of peace – a time to reflect and be grateful. Yet even now if he could prevent his departure he would. The prospect of leaving brought only sadness and uncertainty. The reason for going seemed far away, from a different world, a painful world. But the purpose for which his heart had chosen forced him to go. He knew the Valley would always be part of him. And yet he could never quite suppress the feeling that he'd been caught in a weird and wonderful dream.

Then again, he thought, *perhaps it was not a dream, but a hidden reality – that there is, in truth, a perfect world – a world where fear and sorrow cannot exist.*

Aware of Sami's apprehension, Venus took care to explain: 'Little in the Earth world unfolds as you predict, which makes life difficult – and it's meant to be that way. Hardship forces you to use your creative powers to overcome – for you would not do so otherwise. Braving obstacles is far nobler than retreating to a life of ease, which offers no challenge or goal to strive for. Think back, Sami – think back to your early days and give thought to the words of Apollo: '*you never know what you can do until you have tried.'*

Sami looked undecided. Deep down, he sensed the summons of a great battle and wondered if he was equal and up to the challenge.

'I feel it's time to face my destiny,' said Sami, bravely. 'Please, show me the way home.'

With a smile in her voice, Venus granted Sami's request, 'No need to delay,' she said. 'The sooner you go – the sooner your home.'

Sami expressed his gratitude and deep sense of obligation to Venus and all his Valley friends. He knew how much he'd miss this idyllic world. But regardless of his desire to stay, he was powerless to resist the ever-pressing longing for home.

'In this lifetime, Sami, you have the chance to discover the deepest truth of all – the truth about your *Self*,' said Venus.

'Destiny has great things in store for you. So go – have a safe passage home – let *Truth* be your guide – and may you satisfy your longing for home.'

Then Venus withdrew the light – and like a ghostly vapour the Valley of Awareness and Forgetfulness dissolved into the realms of oblivion, haloed by the golden mist of truth.

The sudden change of scenery startled Sami. *What happened!* he wondered. Then unexpectedly, Pluto appeared, waving one of his limbs, a gesture for Sami to come closer. Sami found it hard to resist the request.

'I have a secret that will cheer your heart,' greeted Pluto.

In a fog of confusion, Sami proceeded towards the octopus. As he drew near, Pluto released an inky-black mist, engulfing him in a blinding cloud. Sami kept calm, however, despite his sightless condition. Although he could not see he could still hear – and he heard a voice – a soothing, reassuring voice: 'All of heaven's creations strive upwards and there are no exceptions. When the heart weeps at what it has lost, the spirit laughs at what it has found – *in your end is your beginning.*'

The words echoed and re-echoed in Sami's mind until he lost all track of time. When he finally regained his senses, he found himself suspended in the midst of a silver-blue sea. He breathed like one who had just awakened from a deep sleep after having dreamed a perfect dream. And yet, he could neither recall its beauty nor its details. He felt an unexplainable sadness but also joy – a welling from within, something ecstatic, for he had a definite feeling he was going home. He looked around, trying to find his bearings. He had no idea where he was or how he got to where he was, but of one thing he was certain, and felt with conviction – he was going back to his natal home, the stream of his birth. With eyes full of purpose, Sami flexed his fins, pumped his gills and with a confident kick set course for home.

Homeward Bound

Like billowing waves,
Like the ebb and flow of the sea,
The longing for home cannot be stifled.

In high spirits, Sami embarked on the long journey home, his pace deliberate and nonstop. Instinct ruled and held him on course. Home never left his mind. But as time went by, with only his thoughts for company, doubt crept in and gained control. Instinct ebbed, and then withdrew. Only time advanced. Sami had lost his way.

Several months on, with no sight of home, Sami entered a blue-green sea overly seeded with plant life. Suffering pangs of hunger he scouted the area for plankton, his favourite food. His search soon led him to the edge of a deep sea-trench. Curious by nature he entered and explored. As he nosed down into deeper depths the sea lost its clarity, turning from clear to featureless grey. Filtering through shades of half-light, a surface vessel began to form and take shape. The ship rested on its keel, devoid of life, consumed by decay. Its barnacled masts, upright and sea-worn, swayed gently with the current. A cold chill ran up his spine. He could not shake the feeling that something beyond unpleasant lay in wait. Ignoring the warning, he moved closer to the ship. 'Danger! Danger!'

screamed an inner voice. 'Avoid the ship! Stay away!' Sami's mind pulsed with alarm, compelling him to act. With a sense of urgency, he kicked his tail, desperate to change course. At the same time, dark and menacing, his worst nightmare broke cover. He recognized the head of a shark. It starred with dull, impenitent eyes. Jagged teeth flashed a hollow smile. Sami's dreaded archenemy loomed large and fierce and poised to strike!

'Enjoy your last moment alive!' sneered the shark.

Mordred lunged at Sami, his bone-crushing teeth snapping! Sami felt a cold, sucking rush grab hold. In frenzy, he plunged forward, kicking furiously, frantic to break free. Then he froze in stunned disbelief! A black and white behemoth of enormous proportions materialized before his eyes. Ignoring Sami, the stranger made straight for Mordred, thumping him repeatedly with punishing head butts. Bruised and battered, the shark wobbled dizzyingly, senseless, off balance. The stranger pulled back to assess the damage and the shark's capacity to harm. Mordred tried to steal away. The stranger, however, had other plans. In a terrifying, headlong rush he thundered towards the shark, targeting its soft and vulnerable underbelly. Such a devastating blow was struck that all that remained of Mordred was a badly shattered ego and a highly startled expression. Mordred's reign of terror had come to a sudden end.

'Are you alright, Sami?' asked a friendly voice.

Shaken but none the worse for wear, Sami stammered, 'I'm not sure. I feel a bit queasy – but I think I'm more or less intact – I can still kick my tail and flex my fins.'

'You must learn to listen to the voice within,' scolded the stranger.

'If you'd done so you could have avoided the shark attack!'

Stupefied, Sami stared at a living creature of gargantuan scale – bigger than imagination – truly a phenomenon. 'Who are you?' he gasped. 'And why did you come to my aid?'

'I heard cries of alarm coming from your inner *Self,*' the stranger replied.

'By the way, my name is Keiko. I appear as an Orca – better known as a killer whale.'

Thoroughly unhinged by the shark attack, Sami needed time to settle down and calm his nerves. But he also needed the comfort and company of a friend. 'Please Keiko,' he asked, 'can you stay and keep me company?'

'As much as I'd enjoy your company, Sami, I cannot interfere any further,' replied the whale.

'There are lessons you have to learn on your own.'

'But I'm lost and alone and far from home,' argued Sami.

'Please, stay and keep me company,' he pleaded.

'You may be lost, Sami but you are not alone,' reminded Keiko.

'You have a great mission to accomplish – a great distance to travel. There's no time to waste.'

'Nothing seems to be going right for me,' complained Sami.

'I want to go home but I don't know where it is.'

'If you cannot live out the bad you won't live to see the good,' countered the whale.

'To discover new oceans, you need the courage to lose sight of the shore. You must learn to believe and trust in your *Self* and not lean on doubts and fears. Remember – the sparrow flies in flocks, whereas the eagle flies alone. Like the free-ranging eagle, you must trust your *Self,* and like the river running to join the sea you must be just as determined.' After a thoughtful pause, Keiko continued.

'Life is a maze of puzzles,' explained the whale. 'What appears disconnected on the surface is linked underneath like the caps of waves on the ocean. At the end of the day, you'll look back and see where all the pieces fit, even if you don't see it now. Try not to worry, Sami. Things will work out for the best,' comforted the whale. 'They always do.'

'I hope so,' said Sami, 'I hope so. But I don't know where I am or where I'm going!'

'If you don't know where you're going, then any route will take you there,' said Keiko, lightly.

'But every part of me wants to go home,' cried Sami. 'Please help me!'

'You cannot find your home unless you're prepared to fight for it – there is no easy or fight-free way,' said Keiko. 'If you have no faith in your *Self* – if you have no 'fight' or 'try' in you then don't expect to succeed – you're bound to fail. It's true, Sami, if you fight you can lose but if you don't fight you've already lost!'

'But I am trying,' insisted Sami.

'What more can I do,' he asked.

'I'd give anything to be back home again – please, Keiko, stay and help me!'

'When faced with adversity, Sami, you need something stronger, deeper and longer lasting than an isolated you – you need your *Self* – for *Self* is a powerful force. It parries all blows and rallies the powers of the universe. The more you trust and rely on your *Self* the more you'll recognize and overcome your fears. That's what courage is about –

conquering your fears. Remember, your fear was Mordred's best weapon.'

Keiko paused briefly before he explained: 'Life is tough and demanding and if you give up on your *Self,* you'll never reach your goal.'

Then Keiko's expression turned serious and with passion he said: '*Let Self be a terrifying longing and let that terrifying longing crowd out everything else.*'

And before departure, he emphasized: '*do not dream the possible – dream the impossible.*'

Without further delay Keiko kicked his tail and promptly faded into nothingness, as if swallowed by shadow.

'Goodbye Keiko,' said Sami to an empty space. And in a more subdued tone added a simple but meaningful, 'Thanks.' Although Sami appreciated Keiko and valued his counsel once Keiko was out of sight – he was out of mind. And so, doubt returned. However, when Sami renewed his journey again his mind invariably gravitated towards the power of *Self-belief.* Oddly enough he was sure he'd heard these words spoken before, from someone else. But 'when' and 'where' his mind drew a blank. Shortly thereafter, an inner voice whispered: '*the power is within you.*' Unfortunately, Sami failed to take notice.

Sami had never felt more alone. Apart from his beating heart the silence was total. Not knowing what lay ahead made him uneasy and insecure. His thirst for home was undeniable and yet he hadn't the vaguest notion where it was. Never before had he felt so inadequate, pitting youth, inexperience and his meagre store of wisdom against the uncaring, immensity of the ocean. *Still*, he thought, *home is what I want and home is where I shall go*. And so, with hope in his heart and a goal to strive for, he bravely headed into the future.

Lost and Adrift

'I fear that I'm to be,
Compassed by the whims of the sea,
And that I'll never know another fate,
Then this incessant, wandering, restless state.'

Sami roamed the vast, trackless wastes of the oceans, his course wayward, like a boat with neither mast nor rudder. Each day the same as the day before – each day tinged with despair. There was no sense of gain, only depressing failure. 'I belong to nowhere,' he conceded, sadly. He spent long days tormented by thoughts, thinking and believing that life had no purpose, no meaning. His once boundless energy turned to lethargy. The hopeless look of the forgotten crept into his eyes. He was lost and alone – an isolated light sputtering in a sea of darkness – his prospects bleak. He soon became prey to obsessive delusions, imagining that he was an unwanted alien who had strayed off course and ended up on planet earth. At odds with reality, he was convinced that failure and disappointment were the laws of life. With eyes fixed on vacancy, he raged inside his mind, at war with the universe. The ocean simply heaved a sigh, as unconcerned as the distant shore.

Sami's journey, going nowhere, dragged on with no end in sight. The longer home eluded him, the fewer the clues, the deeper the mystery. Irretrievable time fled into the past. Now and then, when least expected, half-memories of home would flit through his mind, giving a glimpse but nothing more. In time, he became one of many who slip their moorings and drift aimlessly with the current, lacking destination or purpose. With sunken spirit, he lamented, 'All I have is a chain of intolerable choices, living in a world I want no part of – there must be more than this?'

Sami's endless quest for home yielded nothing and *Nothing is what I am*, he thought, *nothing but a small, fragile, infinitesimal speck on the face of the universe, powerless and expendable.* And yet, pray tell, how can a candle in the sun know itself as light?

Like a malignant fog a terrible desolation had descended and Sami had no will to resist. 'Don't I mean anything at all,' he moaned. 'I have nowhere to go and a lifetime to get there. Is home worth the effort?' Home, it seemed, was no more than a hollow dream – as remote and inaccessible as a star. No matter how far he travelled – how wide he searched – his future stretched emptily ahead. Yet Sami kept trying, refusing to quit. No sunrise found him where sunset left him. And when the will to carry on was gone, courage was there to light the way – and so he followed.

One day, deep in the sky, a silver bird picked up sounds of sadness, echoing from Sami's heart. From a distance, the bird followed Sami, sharing his loneliness. They were strangers on different paths but bound for the same port.

Heart-sad and lonely, Sami lived his life like a song out of tune. Centuries, years, days – how many passed, he no longer cared. Lost and adrift he languished in despair; 'To find the undiscoverable I have all of eternity and the rest of time,' he sighed. Every day buried a yesterday and every day buried his hopes. Yet hope became his beacon light. It's the last of our feelings to wither and die and deep in Sami's heart a tiny ember still flamed.

During this troubling spell of self-doubt and failure, Sami missed Apollo most of all. *How strange*, he thought, *that the loss of someone close could lead to such terrible loneliness? A single soul is missing – a loyal friend – a trusted guide – and life becomes unbearably empty.*

My shepherd is missing.
I am in want ...
Alone,
Untended,
A faraway planet
Forgotten by the sun,
Abandoned,
Lost,
The homeward trail
Unfound,
Weary, bewildered,
Forsaken,
My light grows dim.

Yet Sami was not alone. The sea, the constantly changing sea spoke to him in its ceaseless rhythm. It spoke a single wave at a time, cajoling, caressing, urging him on. Something was always at work behind his mind and in times of adversity he heard it like a tender love song. It eased his pain and soothed his aching heart.

In the reaches of the heavens a kindred spirit stirs. From the hollows of the cosmos a lightless star ignites. Upon a barren ocean a lonely bell buoy tolls. And somehow, somewhere, something draws – beyond powers to resist – a half-remembered lake – a long forgotten stream – the shadow of another place – the golden dream of home.

Sami harkened to the whisper of a wandering echo, 'Even a tiny flame cuts through a thick darkness.'

The waves murmured, 'The darkest hour is just before the dawn.'

At low volume the ocean intoned, 'There's always a way when desire is coupled with courage.'

Shortly thereafter, sporadic glimpses of starry skies and crescent moons kept drifting in and out of Sami's mind – spectacular scenes that suggested time would make things right – would somehow lead him home.

Meanwhile, in the deep blue yonder, Apollo paused to ponder, 'my long-lost dragonfly hunter, what place have you got to, I wonder …'

Turning Point

'Believe in your Self'

A light pierced the blue of the sky. The light grew brighter as it drew closer and soon became a pure white albatross. The bird glided downwards towards the sea and settled on a rolling wave. It rode the ocean swell like a royal prince, watchful and regal. Moments later Sami arrived. The bird radiated love and compassion, 'Sad soul, take heart in knowing the sunrise has never failed us yet.'

Sami braked to a sudden stop. Flecks of light sparkled the sea. An invisible cord of tenderness stretched from albatross to Sami. Sami raised his eyes to peer through a haze of blue and beheld an imposing bird all feathered in white. The image gave rise to a similar bird of long ago, gliding across a misty mountain lake.

'Lost souls like you, Sami, often ask themselves what they are doing here,' greeted the bird. 'And just like you they find their lives to be meaningless. Adversity is the first path to truth. You are lost for good reason for it forces you to ask deep and penetrating questions – it impels you to keep probing and searching for meaning. And in the end, you will find it.'

Sami listened, transfixed, his attention undivided.

'On your journey of self-discovery, you've travelled far and wide and faced difficult trials fraught with danger,' acknowledged the bird.

'But bear in mind, Sami, in this world, suffering is the one promise life always keeps. So, if by chance happiness comes your way accept it as a precious gift to be held and cherished for a brief time only.'

'I've suffered most of my life,' admitted Sami, sadly. 'Won't I ever know happiness again? Will I ever find my home? I thought time would make things right.'

'Yes – but time can also reveal the truth,' replied the bird – 'let yesterday's pain be your strength. You cannot know the good unless you've known the bad. Those who have sunk to the deepest depths are those that have risen to the greatest heights. Every unpleasant experience, every failure and every physical pain carries with it the seed of an equivalent benefit.'

'I'm as mixed-up and confused as ever,' confessed a discouraged Sami.

'I'm lost and alone and trapped in a world I never made. I have power over nothing. I'm so weary of the struggle. When will it end? I'd rather have a single drop of luck than an ocean full of wisdom. I have no choice but to trust in the treachery of the future.'

As he opened his heart to the stranger it dawned upon him that he knew not to whom he was speaking. 'You are a stranger to me. Who are you?'

'I am known as Proteus,' said the bird. 'I appear as an albatross – a bird of the sea. I have found that which is greater than wisdom; the flame of spirit within your heart ever gathering more of its *Self.*'

'I don't understand,' said Sami.

‘Your pain and suffering have not gone unnoticed,’ said Proteus. ‘A small but growing awareness of *Self* is springing from your heart. It won’t be long before you’re fully aware. Then all will change for the good.’

Sami looked puzzled. He was unaware of his awareness of *Self*.

‘Do you recall the Valley and an Angel called Venus?’ asked Proteus.

‘No, I don’t think so,’ said Sami.

‘I don’t remember any Valley and I certainly don’t know of an Angel called Venus,’ he added.

‘Over the course of your journey you once paid a visit to the Valley of Awareness and Forgetfulness,’ reminded Proteus.

‘That’s where you first met Venus, the Angel of Light.’

Sami’s expression clearly showed that he knew nothing about a Valley or of an Angel called Venus.

‘Sorry,’ he said, ‘I just don’t remember.’

And yet the mere sound of the name ‘Venus’ stirred feelings of warmth and kindness.

‘Never mind, Sami. In time you’ll remember,’ Proteus assured.

‘But now listen and understand: everything in life no matter how good or bad comes to an end. Life is all beginnings and endings. Nothing ever stays the same. Know that misfortune never lasts forever. It is only when life is difficult that it becomes meaningful. It is difficulties that show us who we are.’

As he listened to Proteus, Sami searched his mind for lost memories.

‘Be grateful for your Valley visit,’ said Proteus.

‘It was there that the Angel of Light empowered you with the secrets of the universe.’

‘I don’t know if I know what you say I know,’ said Sami.

‘But there is one thing I do know,’ he said with confidence.

‘I want to go home. I’m more sure of this than anything else. Home is my dream my only dream!’

‘The only dreams that are lost are the dreams you don’t fight for!’

‘But I’ve searched far and wide in every place and everywhere – I seem to be going around in circles, going nowhere – I simply don’t know where my home is!’ he cried.

‘I don’t even know where I am – I’m lost – tell me, please – is there a way – a sign – a path I can follow? Please Proteus, I am desperate for home. Tell me, please!’ he pleaded.

‘Home does not appear on any map, only your heart knows the way,’ said Proteus.

‘Follow your dream. Make that dream your life. Let your mind, muscles, nerves and every part of your being be filled with that dream. Let that be all in your heart. Even if your mind tries to deceive you, your heart will whisper the truth. That is the path to victory, Sami – that is the gateway home.’

‘Then please – tell me if I’m near the inland river?’ pressed Sami.

‘I am not the helper you need,’ replied Proteus.

‘Each of us has to be our own hero. Home can only be found by your own efforts.’

‘But where is it!’ cried Sami, exasperated.

‘Please give me a clue – an inkling – a hint – anything, no matter how small or trivial that helps me find home?’

'Your mind alone cannot guide you – only your heart can – for *Self* speaks through the heart – and sometimes what the heart dictates makes no sense – yet it must be followed. Never underestimate the power of your *Self.* To judge your *Self* by its smallest deed is to measure the power of the ocean by a single wave. Let your eyes see with your inner light and behold your true greatness. Infuse your dream with belief in your *Self.*'

It was difficult for Sami to believe in something that gave no visible sign or solid proof. And yet, as he anguished over his dilemma, he knew it made no sense to listen to Proteus and then ignore what he said. Proteus had impressed upon him that without *Self-belief he'd never find his home.* And Sami was desperate to find home. As he searched his mind for answers a well-known voice startled him: '*what you want to know, Sami, is who you are – and who you are wants to know you. Stop searching everywhere and look within.'*

Visions of the Valley flooded through Sami's mind. He recognized the voice of Venus and for Sami to ignore the Angel of Light was unthinkable. 'Proteus,' he asked, 'please help me find my *Self*?'

Sami's sudden reversal of mindset was a welcome relief for Proteus. For Sami's great challenge was fast approaching and he had yet to find his *Self.*

Proteus dipped his head beneath the surface and peered deep into Sami's eyes: 'The time has come to open your heart and welcome your *Self.'* And then he proceeded to unseal the secret: 'To discover your *Self,* Sami, is neither difficult nor complicated: *simply anchor all your belief in your Self,* for *Self feeds on belief. The stronger your belief the stronger Self becomes – and the stronger you become.'*

A glint appeared in Sami's eyes as if a flame, long extinguished, had just rekindled. Sami understood and acknowledged: 'When *I lost my belief – I lost my Self.'*

Before Proteus was on his way, he shared an age-old truth: *'faith is to believe in what you cannot yet see – and the reward of that faith is to see the reality of your belief.'* Then Proteus shared another truth: 'One who has conquered their doubts and fears is a far greater hero than one who has conquered a thousand times a thousand foes. Nothing worth having is ever gained easily. There is always sacrifice. Remember, the dream is what matters – the fight is what it's all about. There is no limit to what you can achieve. Destiny will unfold and champions will rise. Believe in your *Self*, Sami – and you cannot fail!'

With mission accomplished, the albatross swept his wings, lifted off the sparkling sea and melted into thin air as if a snowflake on water.

Darkness Radiates Light

'Lead on, oh kindly light, lead on'

Light dropped a solitary ray into the ocean-sea and held Sami in its glow. A great power enfolded him in arms of tenderness, beauty and understanding. Little by little everything that seemed incomprehensible became simple. Problems that appeared insoluble were resolved. Sorrows, from which he thought he would never recover, vanished naturally. Out of the depths of despair a light had risen to pierce the darkness. Sami saw so clearly how life had led to this moment – had been but a preparation for his journey. *What is it*, he thought, *that so binds me to my destiny?* He felt no sensation of decision, his response no more of choice than the sun rising on a new day.

Sami had but one purpose in mind, one aim and one desire only, which fired his dream and every moment of his waking day. Home alone made his day shine bright and the morning glow with hope.

Stardust sprinkled down and kissed the ocean-sea, sowing seeds of light to mark the homeward trail. With the euphoria of hope resolve sharpened, purpose flooded back and aimless wandering evaporated as completely as a windswept cloud.

The light tracked a given ocean line with undeviating exactitude. With thrilling urgency, Sami powered ahead of the following sea, his progress rapid and sure. With unfailing discipline, his tail kicked to the beat of his heart. Confidence grew with each passing mile, the distance steadily rewound. Like a master mariner, he skilfully navigated the oceans of the world. His tireless strength lay in the force of his will – the certainty of his purpose.

Sami was alone and yet not alone. He was constantly aware of a mystical force hovering within, an ethereal spirit urging him on. He sensed its majesty, its power, and was content to yield to its authority.

Sami's homeward journey passed trouble-free, almost without incident. But then one day as the sun flooded the sea with light, a fascinating sight captured his eye. Close to the surface, sparkling like diamond dust, swarmed an extraordinary concentration of herring. They moved with the current, drifting like a cloud, feeding on clumps of algae. In need of nourishment, Sami chose to join them.

Human Encounter

'A one-sided affair'

A strange, intrusive noise vibrated throughout the depths, violating its soundless nature. The herring tensed. Sami was acutely aware of danger but not of its kind. The low, rumbling growl rapidly increased, then deepened and grew suddenly deafening. Something was wrong – terribly wrong! The buffeting roar, horrifying in intensity, triggered waves of shock in every direction. Marine life panicked and scattered, frantic to flee the unnatural sound. All at once, the frightened fish moved as one. Large numbers of sea-life were gathered en masse and hauled up to the surface. Sami was part of the haul. Crammed to suffocation, he rose higher and higher – the sea turned lighter and brighter – his gills choked on air. Why could he not break free?

As Sami broke the surface – a sharp, blinding flash shattered his day into a millions of pieces. His body turned sluggish – like lead. Taken by a predator – unknown – he was forcefully dragged, semi-immersed, through the churning wash of the cruellest beast of all – a sinister, powerful, menacing monster that plundered the depths of the sea from the heights of his world. Cunning and utterly ruthless, the floating monstrosity stalked its prey – relentlessly – day in, day out – its aim and purpose, deliberate – its thirst for blood, unquenchable – its capacity for slaughter, unrivalled. Peculiar looking figures clambered over its body. Panic seized his mind. Furiously he fought, raging to be free. Sami needed help and he desperately needed it now!

As if from nowhere an enormous enormity appeared in a blaze of polished steel. Charged with purpose, loaded with power, its huge bulky frame moved like lightening, its pent-up strength begging for an outlet. A long, spiralled tusk, like a tapered spear, extended far out in front of its face. The stranger made straight for Sami, intent on shredding the inhibitive web. The constraining meshwork was attacked with such force and precision that all that remained were a few tangled threads. With a flurry of kicks the imprisoned cargo bolted for the open sea, racing off to freedom.

Once the initial shock had settled, Sami slowed down to collect his thoughts. The horror of the occasion had left a troubling impression, which made him curious about his assailant as well as his benefactor. By now he'd come to believe and accept that unseen forces were hard at work, shielding him against harm and foul play. He sensed the latest caller was part of this phenomenon. After taking stock of his surroundings Sami confirmed, with a wave of relief, that he was free and clear – safe and sound. At this time, his defender appeared by his side.

'It seems you can never get enough of what you don't want,' greeted the visitor, light-heartedly. 'You're fortunate I arrived in the nick of time. I appear as a Narwhal – the unicorn of the sea. My name is Nimrod.'

The encounter had been a harrowing and unforgettable experience for Sami, which left him badly shaken. All the same, he managed to show his appreciation. 'Thank you, Nimrod,' he said, simply.

'No need to thank me, Sami, the pleasure is all mine,' replied Nimrod.

'Things are never so bad that they can't get worse,' he cheerfully added.

'Today you've met and confronted the most confounding species the universe has ever produced – Homo Sapiens. Also known as humankind, these air-breathing primates belong to a different order of creation than you. Not higher, necessarily, just different. Humans live in the world of air, which exists above the surface, while we live beneath the surface in the world of water. Over time, the human species has evolved into a class by itself, unequalled in creative powers. However, humans do have a dark side – they are erratic and find cruelty appealing. It is only mankind with its unique power of imagination that takes pleasure in another's pain – the only species to seek revenge and kill for sport – and the only species when faced with adversity, are prone to self-destroy. Mankind represents the universe's highest achievement and yet, ironically, are its worst enemy. There are exceptions, of course.'

'They seem like a cruel and heartless species to me,' admitted Sami.

'And should be avoided altogether,' stressed Nimrod. 'They pose as one of the major threats to your destiny. The earth world, as you've come to know, is a dangerous and complex place. And when you see the full extent and nature of its human inhabitants, you'll find that there's nothing quite so difficult to define. Humans are capable of so much good and yet in the same breath can turn and break each other's spirit, destroying the will to live. Every living creature without exception, is worthy of *kindness, compassion and tolerance*. The unwillingness of the human species to honour and respect this universal law has condemned most of its kind to a life of misery, burdened with hardship and untold suffering. Mankind's greed and lust for power, its insatiable addiction to violence, its lack of empathy along with its failure to provide enlightened and visionary leaders bodes ill for the species and its survival. In truth, we are all one and the same, children of the universe.'

'Since we are all members of the universal family, then why do humans do the things they do and cause so much pain and suffering?' asked a puzzled and thoughtful Sami.

'Humankind live in a world dominated by trauma, hardship and catastrophe, no different than you,' explained Nimrod.

'And just like you, they seek truth and also share your longing for home. But in their struggle to prevail they fail to see the havoc they wreak. Mankind is impatient for truth to emerge and yet resist it when it does – they pursue knowledge only to deny it. Arrogance and blinding ignorance misleads them. Their lives are mired in a maze of confusion where fact and fable have become so profoundly muddled that extracting truth is near to impossible. Many humans, if not most, are rooted in false beliefs and have yet to recognize that everything in this world is connected and there is nothing that exists in isolation. As a result, they cannot see the wisdom in which each life is considered sacred and worthy of the highest dignity. At this stage of their evolution, mankind has far to go. So, keep your distance, always be wary – never be off-guard.'

Nimrod's eyes visibly brightened as he next announced, 'I have good news for you, Sami. You're on the threshold of the inland waterway – the river that takes you home.'

This indeed was welcome news. With morale boosted, Sami again thanked Nimrod and promised to steer clear of mankind. However, unsettled by his human encounter he appealed to Nimrod to accompany him to the river. Nimrod readily agreed for unlike Sami he knew the trials that lay ahead. Thus, the two set out together, the unicorn and his charge, advancing towards the river, the last obstacle that stood between Sami and Home.

The following day, at break of dawn, Nimrod slowed to a halt. 'The time has come for us to part company,' he said.

'Not to worry, though,' he added. 'A guide called, Malachi, will appear shortly. He will escort you as far as the river. Pay heed to his counsel.'

Before parting, Nimrod turned to Sami and in a voice filled with emotion, let it be known: 'Be strong and of good courage; be not afraid or dismayed; for I am with you always, wherever you are.' Thereupon, the unicorn began to dim and fade into the background and soon vanished altogether.

Nimrod's timely intervention along with his wisdom and insight on humankind had left a deep and lasting impression, which Sami knew he'd never forget. Nor would he forget the fear and horror of his one-sided confrontation with the human species. But right now, more than anything, he looked forward to going home.

In less than a day, true to Nimrod's word, the familiar tang of offshore waters began to flow and filter through Sami's gills. In happy anticipation, his heart beat faster.

Final Briefing

'Forewarned is forearmed'

Sami was making good progress, closing in on the river, when all at once the sea welled up and radiated in a fiery glow. At the same time, a prodigious and commanding figure shimmered into existence. Abruptly, Sami braked to a stop. 'Could this be my new guide?' he wondered. At first glance, the stranger looked similar to the otter, Loki, which made him less uneasy. Even so, there was a huge difference. His size was considerably larger and he also possessed two imposing tusks that curved down from his upper jaw. Although his manner was relaxed, overall, he appeared a bit pompous. Right from the start, Sami found himself the critically inspected target of deep-thinking eyes, which gave the impression of examining him with an all-knowing intelligence. An anxious moment ensued. Sami relaxed only when the stranger made known his name.

'I am Malachi,' grumbled a low, gravelly voice.

'I appear as a walrus,' he announced.

'I've come from far, far away – far beyond the horizon, from the deepest mists of time. Listen closely to what I say. You're on the brink of your greatest challenge – the inland river leading home – the most difficult and dangerous part of your journey. But for you to achieve your destiny and make your dream a reality you'll have to employ all your skills and more. Take heart, though, for your great struggle is nearly over. But to reach home and claim victory you must hold your vision with an iron grip and be prepared to go beyond the outermost limits of strength and endurance.'

Sami treaded water while he listened to Malachi. His spirits were high. He felt the most difficult and dangerous part of his journey was behind him. Compared to ocean navigation, the river seemed of little concern. During his long and difficult journey, he'd escaped death and disaster on numerous occasions. He thought, *Whatever could not destroy me only made me stronger*. His global ventures had taught him valuable lessons. So why shouldn't he be pleased with himself? He could swim the river with ease; after all, he'd done it before. The possibility of failure did not exist. The future looked bright – the outcome assured.

Noting Sami's thoughts, Malachi scowled and shot him a piercing glare. In a voice sharp with authority, he said: 'Let's be clear, Sami – you'll not succeed unless you're prepared for a hard and heavy duel. Few survive the upriver run. You cannot begin to comprehend the difficulties you'll face. The river preys on everyone seeking home. She is known for her ruthless reputation – her awesome blend of power and innovation. To go the distance and reach home you'll have to give the performance of a lifetime – relying on strength, resolve, and above all, courage.'

Humbled by Malachi's rebuke, Sami apologized.

'I'm sorry,' he said.

'I didn't think the river would be a problem. It wasn't before.'

Then out of interest he asked, 'Please, Malachi – explain courage to me?'

Malachi's features softened as he carefully mulled over his response: 'Courage,' he said, 'is the difference between success and failure, between victory and defeat. It means facing the challenge before you when you know there is little chance of success.'

Malachi understood the value of courage and knew the dominant role it would play. He had yet to be convinced that Sami was equal to the challenge. The upriver run was long and fierce and in the end, it would be up to Sami alone. Sami must search his mind and discover what is true – that courage has always been part of him. This was crucial. And so, Malachi revealed the following: 'Sami, have you ever wondered what's hiding inside you? When first you came into this world the seed of courage was planted in your heart. Soon you will discover the power it holds. That which seems so small and feeble in you is destined to be the strongest and most determined.'

'What are you saying?' cried Sami.

'That I've always had courage! I'm not sure I follow. Please explain – tell me more.'

'Courage has played a major role from the very start of your existence,' explained Malachi.

'It stems from your inner *Self* and acts on your behalf for your greater good only. That's why *Self-belief* is such a fearful force. It does not depend on outer resources. It's not so much your outward power that matters – it's the power within that counts. Learn from the stars in the heavens – only an inner explosion allows them to shine. Hope for the best, plan for the worst – use fear as an engine – not a brake – make pain your teacher, not your master. With a vengeance you must be like a dragon slayer – a fearless warrior instilled with an all-consuming will to win. The task before you requires nothing less. Winning or losing lies only within you. Rely on and trust only your *Self.*'

Sami kept silent, taking in every word.

'Time is not your friend,' said Malachi. 'Your moment is now! What price are you willing to pay to make your dream come true? How will you perform when you're overtasked, severely impaired and near collapse? What will you do when the strain and pain is so great that your mind quits and your body screams in protest? Can you keep going when it seems impossible to do so?'

Sami's confidence wavered. 'I don't know,' he stammered.

'I've never faced anything so drastic before.'

'Is it in you to focus your attention on one perfect dream?' pressed Malachi.

'Have you the inner strength to dare to fail? Have you the grit to turn defeat into victory? Have you the will to do whatever it takes, to risk everything for a dream that nobody sees but you?'

'Home is never outside my heart,' cried Sami with passion.

'It is my dream, my only dream. As long as I have breath in my body – a beat in my heart – there is nothing I won't do to make my dream come true. I'll brave every obstacle, every danger. I will never, ever, ever give up. And that's a promise!'

While Malachi counselled and encouraged Sami, a few of his kind emerged from the ocean depths. Others followed in rapid succession. Before long, their ranks had swelled to a formidable army. The traffic became so thick and full that the sea soon glittered with silver. Brimming with naïve confidence, the salmon jostled for position, eager to enter and conquer the river.

Upon their return, the salmon had altered dramatically. Against his kindred kind, Sami stood out in solitary splendour. Every part of him looked and performed like a lean-muscled missile of the sea.

Sami carefully observed his fellow kind and wondered if any of them had experienced the same things as he had. Then again, he thought, *probably not*. Sami sensed that he alone had faced the great unknown and seen things meant for his eyes only.

Malachi furrowed his brows in deep concentration as he offered a few last words of encouragement, 'As you go forth to challenge the river go in confidence and go with my blessings, but make no mistake, Sami: victory belongs to the one with the strongest will. So do your best – let will and action be in harmony – and hurry home.'

His eyes weighted with wisdom, Malachi concluded: 'In farewell I say unto you – never lose sight of your dream – never stop trying – and never doubt your *Self*!' Before Sami could respond, Malachi began to fade as if dimming his own light and soon disappeared into the mists of time.

As Sami joined forces with his fellow seekers a voice from within whispered: *'true greatness is when you become what you seek!'*

The Home Stretch

'Rough is the road to greatness'

Like an army of exiled heroes, the salmon gathered in a quiet coastal cove, near the river's mouth. Over the following days they foraged the rich, kelp-filled waters in preparation for the trial ahead. Sami also spent time searching for lost companions. Sadly, his efforts brought little comfort. He was one of only a few from his natal stream. Dejected, he swam off to be on his own and consider the warnings of Malachi. As he weighed the risks of the river challenge, the sun sank deep into its bed. A waveless serenity reigned over all. Tomorrow would soon be now.

In the cold, pre-dawn waters a ghostly shimmer of salmon slipped silently into the river's mouth. With minds fixed on home, spirits ran high. The outflow shouldered along with a dull pewter shine, barely offering resistance. Streaks of flesh and scale muffled in smoky gold followed one another like soldiers on parade. Ocean-hardened and travel-wise, the salmon set themselves to blaze a trail with immortal determination, supremely confident that no power on earth could stop the combined force of muscle, instinct and resolve. Energy radiated like an electric charge. With unremitting zeal, Sami rushed towards the crowning achievement of his life.

Homing steadily upstream, the salmon advanced with relative ease. The unhurried drift lulled and seduced, pretending to be harmless. With sharp precision, they cut through the mild counter flow. But before long, tremors of unease began to trickle into the mainstream – the initial warning of an oncoming storm. For the moment, however, the river remained peaceful – her spirit in hibernation.

Filled with the euphoria of home, the salmon set a brisk pace. But soon their headway began to slow. A deep, panting murmur simmered beneath the surface – a miasma of ill-omen. Inspirited by the nearness of home, Sami knifed the current like a well-honed sabre. Strength developed as need arose. He met obstacles undauntedly.

It began as a faint roar, like the sound of surf in a seashell. No longer broad and serene, the river had narrowed her width and showed signs of resistance. Further upriver, the surface vibrated out of rhythm. Loose currents tightened and flexed powerful muscles.

Taut with power the river trembled with unease, her texture in artless disarray. The unannounced intrusion had aroused her anger. Displeasure soon made its presence felt. The pressure intensified. Conflicting currents collided then braided around a fragmented mainstream. Angry welts streaked the surface. The steady hum of willpower grew deeper and more ominous.

The river understood the realities of power. She calibrated her authority up a notch, causing her pulse to beat with a fierce, accelerated rhythm. She'd become a sterner, wilder thing, darkly a-swirl with warlike currents. The salmon sensed an ever-rising path – swimming uphill, against the natural flow.

Sami did not underestimate the scale of the task. The challenge was huge. Mindful of Apollo, he kept repeating – *I am strong – I am not weak – I am strong – I am not weak …* Meanwhile, marshalled in the background, the river's main force hunkered down and waited, poised to pounce with gales of fury.

With a loud cracking boom, the river's latent power surged to life. Full of dash and green flash she burst upon the salmon in a crescendo of violence. Jagged rocks, like broken teeth, cut sharply through her rampant flow. The sudden onslaught caught the salmon unawares. A battle of prolonged intensity was underway.

Cruising the sky, the eyes of an eagle widened in desperate concern as they followed the river far into the distance, suggesting intolerable trials to come.

The river grew more muscular. Her vengeance roared of shores uptorn and living souls devoured. Suppressed anger exploded raw and harsh and black with menace – a blind, colossal, ungovernable force that lashed and slashed and smashed and crashed with unabated leaping rage.

White with fury the whip-lashed river bulldozed a speedway to the sea and the turmoil that followed turned placid water into raw aggressive energy. Churning like the pistons of a speeding locomotive she howled through the narrows like a runaway train. Solid bedrock quivered and quaked from a punishing arsenal on the warpath. Lofty hollow canyons echoed her roars.

Harried from all sides, Sami bore down, driving hard, madly kicking his tail. His kicks were fast and wild. Caught in a shattered world of confusion he toiled as if toil were life itself. Surging water struck as solid as a wall. Shockwaves shoved him up against the spurs of rocks. Spikes of pain peppered his sides. The river played with his agony; maddened fingers clawed his body; each surge charged with anger – each instant filled with malice – progress slowed to a standstill. The home stretch symbolized the ultimate challenge; indeed, it defined the essence of life itself.

The salmon settled into a relentless, muscle-straining procession. They hiked like weary soldiers under an endless reign of terror. By punishing degrees, the strain began to tell. The current grew denser – the path more steep – yet none fought without conviction.

The river has many weapons upon which to draw. And the roiling, boiling cataracts were second to none – a narrow, rock-choked lane of wall-to-wall chaos where each foot gained brought a surge of anger in retaliation. Yard after gruelling yard fresh attacks were mounted, each designed to outdo its predecessor. Sami was singled out, swept aside and pummelled and hammered as hard as an anvil. His eyes glazed with the agony of travail. Each muscle racked by pain; each nerve burned like fire. What he breathed was air and spray and water commingled. Like a prehistoric beast the river roared her defiance, revelling in the torment inflicted – and spread it thick with rapturous fury. Sami's progress slowed as if tunnelling through mud.

A dim twilight brooded over the scene of battle and low in the sky the sun smouldered, draped about with blood-red mists. Against a fleet of storm-bound clouds, the eagle, Horus stood out in silhouette. Beneath his wings raged a serpentine chaos of movement – a thundering deluge of fury, racing inside a chute of jagged rocks and ledges with multiple roaring cataracts thrust between rock-walled turns so sharp that the water, whirling in them, seemed to smoke. Sami was soon to face dread and despair and a vision of hell!

The river sharpened her claws. Slabs of granite, like rough misshapen tombstones, spun water into vicious corkscrewing swirls. Tortured water twisted and flared electric green. Blitzing water forged iron fists of fury, pummelling the salmon with hard, uncushioned blows.

Determined to impose her will, the river goaded the current into homicidal alliance. Now and then the violence would ease, as her fury seemed to inhale – only to return with redoubled force. The river wielded her wild unruly rage with an almost human cunning.

The voice of the river was the devil's choir – a low echoing, haunting roar that growled beneath the surface: *'I see you coming closer – with glory in your sight – if you expect to beat me – be best prepared to fight!'*

On and on with no relief – racing hearts – numbing minds – the smell of panic plaguing the run. Sami pitched and wallowed as his body thundered in protest, his heart hammering against his ribs.

Chronic fatigue consumed them. There was no respite, no momentary lull to gain their strength or let the weary lie easy. The iron resistance only hardened Sami's resolve. Life or death depended on his efforts alone. Nature had neither eyes nor ears nor hands to help.

Sami made no concession to tiredness. Ferociously he kicked his tail, driven by an inner source that spurred beyond fatigue. But as the battle wore on and the violence grew worse his strength began to wear. And still he faced unending miles of mountain river rage.

The distant drumbeat of the warring foe sent icy chills through thumping hearts. The salmon grew edgy, their nerves heightened. They sensed a great challenge yet to be met.

The low rumble of thunder deepened into a loud resounding roar that shook the earth itself. Looming ahead and blocking the way stood a thunderous powerhouse of mass destruction – a wall of terror whose dominating height soared to evaporate high in the sky. Impending doom rolled over the wall and plunged down to crash and mushroom into monstrous heaps – water tumbled out of water – chaos struck from everywhere at once – dread and panic ran rampant. Sami clung on tenaciously, frantically kicking his tail, straining every part of his body – his dream fast sinking in the fury of the falls.

With dread, pain and growing fatigue, the salmon pressed on with grim, instinctive strength. They fought with such devotion to purpose there wasn't room left for fear. Unstoppable tons of glacial melt barrelled over the wall and thundered down to crash with devastating effect. How many tons lay armed and waiting? Sami imagined inexhaustible numbers. The salmon endured a punishing gauntlet of purgatory – a hydro-sonic arsenal blasting every which way that mauled and maimed with its own godlike violence.

From shore-to-shore, nature groaned and shuddered and felt the horrid roar. The river had orchestrated her anger into a great symphony of destruction. Like a mindless beast, she devoured the gallant salmon and drank their blood and tears. Her appetite never sated. Casualties ran heavy. The sickness of hope deferred raged in many hearts. Anticipation of home crumbled into disenchantment and failure. Battle weary and in decline, Sami could barely hold on. Was he the only listener to a sea of anguished cries? Beset by despair, he railed, 'We live in a savage world of pain and suffering!' How could he defeat this tireless battle-ram that barred the passage home? Doubt and fear crept in and clouded his mind. Despite all the skill and ability at his command, Sami questioned whether he'd ever see home again.

In reckless abandon, the salmon tried jumping the wall, only to be driven back in riotous confusion. Kicking hard and fast they leapt like fearless daredevils' time and time again – desperate charges where walls of thunder threw them back – where death fell in showers – and where the river swallowed them up and spat them out in scorn and defiance. It was like rolling a giant boulder uphill and every time you got close to the top down it would roll again. Fatigue lay heavy on heaving hearts. For many, the strain was more than could be borne and the river churned with the last of their failing strength. Others fell back in a desperate string, exhausted, consumed by their efforts – a bloodied army in tatters. With spirits broken, untold numbers went forth as sheep in the midst of wolves – their fragile hopes shattered against the iron gates of adversity.

Sami's heart pumped nothing but terror. Directly ahead, lording dominion over all towered the insurmountable wall. All the courage and resolve of which he was capable crystallized into a single moment. In one tremendous, spontaneous burst, he kicked his tail with all the strength he possessed. Up – up – and up he kicked – up through the heavy, headlong plunge – up through the barrier of his burning pain – up through the dreaded fear of failure – and with a backbreaking do-or-die kick reached and breached the crest at the top. But alas, like an arrow launched, it was too late to alter flight. Imperilled in a blinding, pressure less space, Sami hung naked and defenceless in the thin mountain air.

So close was Sami, so close to conquering the unconquerable wall that he was horribly shocked when the unexpected struck. A sweeping blow toppled him shoreward, sending him somersaulting, end-over-end in wild disorder. Sheets of pain rippled through his body – water burst from his gills – and the world spun out of orbit as he pitched blindly over the falls and crashed down on the rocky shore beyond. The sudden shock of air immersion left him impotent, gasping for breath.

With eager strides, flesh-eating carnivores converged upon the feeding grounds. Fuelled by hunger, driven by instinct, they waded through the shallows to devour what the river had not yet claimed. Death strode from shore to shore with lethal, sweeping scythes. Claws flayed – fangs tore – gullets engorged. It was anarchy – pure annihilation. Littered with dead the river ran murder-red – a crimson tide of slaughter. Salmon losses were staggering. For Sami, lying helpless and disabled, the roar of the battle diminished to the roll of distant thunder. Against all probability he was still alive but the certainty of death seemed merely postponed. With frantic kicks, he fought in vain, desperate to regain the river. Drowning in air, his chest heaved and writhed for energy denied. As he gasped out his life, severe muscular contractions attacked his body till he is all-aquiver, thrashing in silent torment.

Voracious bears, dripping red from tooth and claw, reared up and roared and gnashed their teeth. A sick realization the end was near flooded through Sami. He'd overcome one deadly danger only to face another.

The eyes of a high-flying eagle zeroed in on the carnage below. Horus shot out of the sun like a feathered bolt of lightning, screeching cries of menace more piercing than a screaming sawmill. Caught off guard, the grizzlies flinched then froze in their tracks.

With pinpoint precision, Horus swooped down and plucked the hapless Sami out and away from grasping claws and yawning jaws. As flapping wings carried him higher and higher Sami feared that his journey had ended – that his efforts had failed. But moments later, to his immense surprise and relief, the eagle's grip sprang loose. Filled with terror and exhilaration, he was free and clear, falling in open air. Before splashing down, Sami heard Horus call out:

'Failure is not final – it's the courage to go on that counts – trust your Self.'

The full force of the current tore into Sami at astonishing speed, sweeping him back towards the crest of the falls. The lightning pace whipped him over the edge where he plummeted head over tail, down into the roiling storm below. The aftermath left him numbed and dazed, barely with life, drifting unresistingly like a feather in the wind. Insensible and disempowered, the current drove Sami further downriver in the opposite direction to home.

Somehow Sami maneuverer through a maze of swirling eddies and jagged rocks. By luck and sheer effort, he'd managed to scramble out of catastrophe, finding refuge in the calm of a slack water pool. Miraculously, he was back in his natural element, alive, able and willing, even though weak fearful and bullied. He knew how narrow his escape had been.

Desperately, he needed time for his battered system to recover. He was painfully aware that he'd failed. The scale of the challenge was fraught with impossibilities. Reluctantly, Sami confessed, 'The fighting foe has lain me low.' Yet his stubborn nature refused to quit – his unbroken will persisted. 'I have given my best and did not succeed,' he admitted. 'I have lost a battle.' But by now Sami had grown worldly-wise, knowing that no one wins all the time. It was the thought of failure, a wasted life that pumped up the inner resources needed to win. He sensed the river was made to test his valour – to measure his force of will. 'The river has many thoughts, I have but one,' he reasoned. 'My one thought, in the end, will prove stronger than the many.' Sami could only be true to himself. He was going home to his natal stream. Or he was going to die trying. He was not going down to an easy defeat.

Although badly outdone and denied his goal, Sami sensed he still had a small but vanishing chance of reaching home. The battle, he thought, may be lost – his journey ended. But experience had taught him that what the eye takes in does not necessarily tell the whole story. Appearance can be misleading. For the river had not attained her goal. She'd failed to take the weary, battle-stricken Sami unto herself.

'I must find a way to win, to turn defeat into victory,' said Sami to himself. Even though every muscle danced with strain, his inner strength remained calm, like the centre of a storm. He understood the value of persistence. Vitality had dimmed, but wisdom gained had balanced out physical loss. As he focused on home, his mood turned defiant. The fear of defeat had given rise to a furious surge of anger. Sami was going on the offensive. Against an onslaught of resistance, he kicked his tail and headed for home.

In a state of desperate purpose, Sami stiffened his resolve and summoned up his strength. But as he laboured towards the core of the roar, his muscles burned like fire and his heart seemed too small for the task. Although hunger for home was fierce and intense, this alone would not see him through. Sami's only hope – his only chance – was to believe in his *Self* and extend the limits of courage.

Regardless of courage, however, the performance of Sami's body was winding down, intolerably moving in slow motion. Doubts assailed him and there was pain, but he kept pain at a distance and fought down his rising fears. Wounded, exhausted and yet unwavering, Sami strained, stretched and quivered on his passionate quest for home.

The perceptive river sensed Sami's re-emerging resolve. Inflamed to extremes, she amassed her aggression with vindictive ferocity, bludgeoning him unmercifully. His body staggered and rebelled. No longer could he rival her energy and drive. The sledge hammering blows had taken their toll, had worked his heart to bursting and left him weak and riddled with pain. Whether he deserved it or not, Sami only hoped that strength would find him as it had so many times before and by an act of grace lift his pain and fatigue and give him a second chance. He must go on – he had to go on – he could not give up. The impossible will always be the impossible until someone makes it happen. He kept repeating – *I am strong – I am not weak – I am strong – I am not weak ...* The supreme moment was set to strike. Filled with a terrible and unshakable resolve, Sami threw caution aside in a last desperate bid to save his dying dream.

The mind, the seedbed of dreams, where the impossible becomes the possible.

Violence howled all around. From bedrock base to unassailable height, the wall thundered wild with rage, like a fire-breathing dragon with a hundred roaring heads. Defiantly, Sami rose and fell within the fierce demonic flood, goring his way through its madness. Sonic booms opened up like siege guns, triggering a deafening chain of percussion. The shattering impact trembled heart and spine. In spite of energy expended, Sami could not gain speed. His endurance stretched to breaking point. Dead ahead and hollowing the surface, a gaping hole that spun so fast it smoked like a furnace – a downward spiral that knotted and unknotted itself like an endless screw. Its whirling motion funnelled him into its spinning eye – round – round – round he spun – down – down – down he swirled – spinning round and down in a dizzy tailspin of horror.

The unforeseen threatened to deal a deathblow to Sami's dream. In a flash of inspiration, he opened his heart to the universe. Instantly, a beam of light blinked throughout the heavens, searching for help. Wildly out of control, he spun deeper and deeper and in a fever of fear pitched blindly down into a shaft of solid black – the din of the centrifuge roaring in his ears.

Entombed in a chamber of unseparated darkness, Sami faced a cruel and bitter end. But then, inexplicably, the terrible roar receded. Incredibly, the dark began to break apart, permitting something to come forth, something glittery and remote. Sami struggled to make sense of it. But the harder he tried the more elusive it became. He dare not move for fear of losing it. Presently, a light emerged. Sami's eyes were drawn towards a nimbus of white – a brilliant vision cloaked in an aura of light. Its invincible rays penetrated the all-merging darkness. Sheets of light illumined the shadows. A cone of light fastened on Sami. All at once the light became aware and began to speak, speaking directly to him. Gently but firmly the radiant splendour opened his mind and lifted the veil of forgetfulness.

'Welcome, Sami,' greeted the light.

'Venus!' cried Sami, 'Why are you here?'

'I've been waiting for you,' she answered.

'It seems I've been through this before.'

'Yes, you have, Sami. But you have not been beyond.'

'In the darkness, I found something,' said Sami.

'What did you find?'

'My courage!'

'No,' said Venus, 'You found your *Self*.'

Lost for words, Sami simply asked, 'How did I get here?'

'By belief in your *Self* and the ghosts and spirits that have been before,' said Venus. 'All your past and present deeds, whether good or bad, create joyful or sorrowful seeds, which are sown in the field of your soul to be claimed in the future. You're on the verge of reaping the harvest.'

Sami listened to the wonder of it all and sensed an inner part of him slowly turn on its axis. 'The Valley of Awareness and Forgetfulness appeared as if a vision from a dream within; elusive things, like shadows in twilight; essences, subtle but real, embedded in Truth.'

'Be free, Sami – be free!' encouraged Venus. 'Forget your fears – trust your *Self* – and only your *Self*. That is the secret! Rely on that trust to take you home. Then you shall unfold all the potential of your being and be more beautiful, more brilliant, more powerful and more alive than you can now possibly imagine. Nothing shall by any means harm you for I am with you, always,' assured Venus.

She then bestowed a treasure beyond measure. 'Sami, you have not used all your power until you have used mine, for that too, is yours. Your moment of destiny is upon you. So go – press forward – make the bounds of freedom wider yet and may love and belief in your *Self* never desert you.' Then Venus began to recede and as she faded into the distance her voice resounded throughout the heavens: '*Uphold the Power of Truth!*'

Sami entered a tunnel and the tunnel had a light. Powerfully revitalized, he headed for the light. Countering the motion that went before he promptly ascended the spinning eye. Hope and passion burned anew.

The river relied on her frightening power – Sami relied on the power of Self.

The final showdown – a whirling world of opposing forces. The river emptied her arsenal, letting loose with everything she had. Barrage upon barrage of unspent fury rolled over the wall and thundered down her granite chute. Sami was challenged as never before. The fierce, bucking motion tossed and flung him about like a stringless puppet. The staccato boom of the rolling roars – a fusillade of rapid jabs, hammered fast – pounded hard. Bone shattering blows jarred every fibre of his being, sapping his strength but not his will. Sami's sudden emergence had launched a horrorfest of shock and awe, yet the fire in his heart burned all the brighter, empowering his will and spurring him on to a final resolution.

Against an avalanche of terror, Sami edged towards the base of the wall. Dark and foreboding it stood like a tombstone anchored to the sky. The din rose to crescendo – the onslaught reached its zenith. Courage surged in the face of defeat. Tensed muscles readied to spring, 'It's now or never,' cried Sami, as he kicked his tail with a power, he never knew he possessed. His strength was colossal, triggering such a wave of energy that he lifted out of the river's grasp like a missile shooting for the stars. With soaring spirit, he climbed higher and higher, mocking the forces of gravity, till at last he broke free, bursting into sunlit air. The falls fell quickly behind. Sami had cleared the most demanding hurdle of all. His timing was impeccable. *Self-belief* had triumphed over doubt.

Against outrageous odds Sami had subdued the indomitable wall. Yet danger pressed from all around. Down below, the muted roar of a force denied – up above the full roar of an appetite unsated. And once again, Sami faced the horror of a grizzly's lunging teeth. But before the bear could seal his fate, a bold little dragonfly alighted its nose. Distracted by the brazen pest, the bear's jaws missed their mark. Thus did Sami maintain his flight, sailing through the air, unmolested, and with a sigh of relief slipped safely back into the river, beyond the crest of the falls. With strong, aggressive kicks he scythed his way to deeper depths, dodging a gauntlet of snapping fangs and raking claws.

Sami continued to wrestle the current. The courage he showed was too much to imagine, inspiring to behold. Driven by a power beyond his own he went the limit for mile after gruelling mile, combating seething crosscurrents and savage beasts. To Sami it seemed like the battle would never end. But then, little by little the anger eased, resistance gave way and Sami knew that his goal was near. And sure enough, as he rounded the next bend, the cherished waters of home welcomed and soothed his panting gills. Destiny had cast its sure and steady beam. The swamping tidal wave of fury had swelled and burst and gradually ebbed, leaving the battle-scarred Sami shaken by its force, a fire in his spirit. And while he basked in his hard-won victory, the river rolled on and on, pursuing her course to the sea.

Home

'The birth of true greatness'

The distance that remained was familiar ground to Sami. He knew it as well as his own heartbeat. In a constant state of exertion, he pressed on, intent on reaching his birth stream. But soon his headway began to stall. Sami's will consented but his body rebelled. With dwindling strength, his pace slowed to a crawl.

Sami's ordeal continued unabated – an escalation of agony. Piteously, the warrior kicked and strained against an ever-weakening resistance. By now, all his snap and fire had evaporated. Carrion birds circled overhead, then swooped down and struck with their iron beaks, inflicting grievous wounds. Time or death must surely put an end to the river's awful vengeance.

Sami groped, straying one way then another, anyway but backwards, making little progress. With faltering kicks, he struggled through oblivion and by some sense of *Self* found the will to carry on. His hard-spent body and desperate manner belied the heart that beat within. Bone weariness, soul weariness, weariness beyond imagining, yet Sami continued to show a limitless reservoir of courage – an unconquerable heart.

Rippling water mingled with the faint sound of wingbeat. A solitary dragonfly shadowed the surface. Almost broken, Sami lumbered on, at times submerged, other times not. Pain penetrated his whole body.

Sami had been called into existence from nothingness and sustained in life by courage. During his long and formidable journey, he'd survived the enormous plains of far-off oceans, faced death-defying trials and fought the full-blown fury of a river raging for the sea. Now all that remained were the muted roars of a force denied and his worn-out, mortal form.

The passage grew narrow and narrower. The river shrank back into her bed. With the absolute abruptness of a sword slash, the current was chopped off – the surface stilled – the roars quelled. Now a mere stream, she murmured no more than a whisper.

Sami's pain echoed from the bottom of the stream to the ends of the earth and far beyond. Was it the pain of a wasted life? Even though his body told him that he'd lost the battle he still refused to lose heart and give up. It was all or nothing – and so, in his way, he persevered. In time, his path led to a quiet, open space softly lanced by light. The uncommon serenity lent solace to his soul. Increasingly, he became aware of a sense of mounting expectation, the unique excitement a traveller feels on the last homeward stretch of a long and hazardous journey – and his heart stood still at the nearness of his prize.

There then arose one of those silences that occur only in the presence of wonders. A lone figure broke the surface and painstakingly breasted across a shallow gravel bar. It was Sami, weak and unaccompanied. He looked dimmed and clouded, exhausted beyond caring – each breath a laboured effort – each move an extreme test of will. With only the smallest of hopes he struggled through exhaustion, kicking feebly, desperate to reach home before the last grain of strength had run its course. 'I have come as far as I can,' he cried, 'someone, take notice – please favour my cause.' And Nature listened in silence as the sun climbed high in the sky. Its face looked down upon this soul with eyes of reverence and wonder, love and awe.

Sami lay in the shallows without movement, the sun's rays saturating his emaciated body. A dragonfly hovered in the air above: 'have no fear, Sami – for I know the future and it is sound – a faraway shore is reachable from here.' It was his friend and guide, Apollo, urging him on. At the same time, as promised long ago the otter, Loki appeared, 'I'll share your load, oh worthy soul – side-by-side we'll reach your goal.'

Sami's heaving breathlessness disturbed the tranquillity of the stream. He was fighting hard not to die – the draw of breath stronger than death. Darkness was closing in all around. Yet even now as his soul flared out of a frail and fading body, he fought to stay in the light.

Apollo continued to comfort and encourage. With swelling pride, he said: 'Your moment is now, Sami – dreams do come true – you dared, you hoped, you believed, and look what you've become – a Lionhearted Warrior of the Light!'

It came to Sami that his body was dying but not his *Soul*. He had reached the end of the known and his *Soul,* in its infinite clarity, knew that the black of cessation was near – that death was only a passing phase, part of a larger plan. Many waters cannot quench love; neither can the floods drown it. The Angel of Light was guiding him home – a home, he sensed, he'd ventured before – a perfect place in a perfect world.

A shaft of light bisected the stream, and the light spoke, 'The home you seek is springing from your heart. You have proven your courage. Let the Truth set you free.' Venus shimmered into view. 'The time has come to tender the light from me to thee. Never shall you cease to exist, and nothing can change this unchanging reality. Be free, Sami, be free. The present you must end. The future you is just waiting to be born.'

Sami's body radiated a pale blue corona, the light within unwilling yet to die. With failing breath, he gasped, 'Where is the light – the light I long for?'

A short time later and as destined, Sami tasted the sweet waters of home. The mother stream once more cradled her treasure. The life force that had broken the peace so long ago had returned. The task was done – the victory won. The journey had reached its end.

A great hush fell over the stream. Gradually the silence lifted as Nature's praise began to rise, gain momentum, and then on wings unseen ascend the heavenly heights where its tale of courage sounded and resounded throughout the vast, star-spangled hollows of space. Within moments, a silver Starbird appeared and hovered directly above Sami. A single beam of light withdrew from its source and dropped down to encircle the fading warrior – a sign that signalled a life without end – a life free of the cycle of rebirth – a life at one with its *Self.*

Majestically, the Starbird hung motionless in the sky, its wings outstretched. A solemn moment passed before the Starbird descended and settled by Sami's wasted form. Its noble bearing gave the impression that something dramatic was about to occur.

Then all at once it happened!

A sudden sweep of wings and the Starbird lifted in flight, Sami firmly in its grip. Once airborne the Starbird aimed for the sky and began to climb, higher and higher it climbed, deep into the distance and far beyond, blazing a trail of triumph to the heaven's beckoning stars. As it soared out of sight, wondrously, brightening the sky, something rare and beautiful: the liberation of a newborn Star! Great profusions of light burst forth and shot high into the heavens, spreading broadly and vastly, intended not only for the eyes of planet Earth but for the infinite eyes of the universe as well. The seal of bondage had been broken. Sami, the lionhearted warrior, was rushing towards the open arms of his natural home.

A star of light is my destined soul, ascending on a cosmic tide – with longed-for freedom trapped inside – impatient for release. A star of light that rises and grows in Courage – in Wisdom – in Truth – has triumphed over its darkest foes – aspiring to be free. This soaring, seeking, brilliant light at last transcends its earthly bonds to burst in joyous liberty amidst the heavenly stars.

Sami had discovered, as destiny willed, the invincible power of the spirit. Imbued with a force of will that is the essence of a champion, Sami had risen to reach a level of courage that others might equal but never surpass. From small beginnings, great things can happen and today if you are one of those lost and troubled souls who yearn to make real their dreams, for inspiration, simply raise your eyes to the sky. For there you will find, shining strong and free, a lionhearted star, happily ever-aftering in the infinite shoreless blue.

Let's now return to the mountain stream and feast our eyes on a scene of delight. The flow of crisp water sparkles under a cloudless sky – tall slender reeds wave like feathery wands – a whispering breeze caresses the trees as a chorus of birdsong fills the air – now and then the water dimples as salmon break the surface to feed – a dragonfly dips and skips along the glassy veneer – a playful otter flips over on its back, scratches its belly then sighs in satisfaction. Nature wearing a fabric woven of sunshine and stardust and wonder – and everything is as it had been, once upon a time.

James L. Wild
23 September 2022
After Words:

If power goes on, struggle goes on – because power beyond its need can only amass more power, and therefore, can only hoard and guard itself. This is the irony of Sami's victory – power was all and reigned supreme – and yet – powerlessness struggled on and became all. Every great fight has been won by superior willpower wresting victory from the jaws of defeat or upon the narrowest of margins. Sami's extraordinary feat of self-will prevailing over exhaustion, his resolve never to submit and above all, his determination to turn defeat into victory is an inspiration to us all. And when the impossible is made possible we recognize the possibility for the whole world.

The invincible power of the *Self* is that which Sami had come to find. In our brief time of *Life* on Earth, everyone's journey is the hero-fight. If we have the courage to face our demons, or destiny, or whatever it may be, it matters not how high or daunting our aim. By embracing a lion-hearted faith in our *Self* inevitably our struggle will prevail. Lest we forget, all roads lead home, but many are rough and pitted with danger. Great is the need for torchbearers. May these guardians of light be valued as rare and precious gems.